SCI FUTURES

presents

The City
of the Future

SciFutures Presents: The City of the Future
Publisher: SciFutures

©2016 SciFutures Presents: The City of the Future

The following content is copyright ©2016 by its respective authors: Learning to Speak Tiger by Trina Marie Phillips; Love in a Lonely City by Deborah Walker; Light Times by Ari Popper; Houseproud by Laurence Raphael Brothers; LA Loves You by Christopher Cornell; One Bad Apple by Holly Schofield; The Calculus of Trees by Sofie Bird; Chicago Blues by Gary Kloster; Drowned City by Bo Balder.

Published by SciFutures First Edition: April 2016

This book is a work of fiction. Names, characters, places and incidents are products of the author's imagination or have been used fictitiously and are not to be construed as real. Any resemblance to persons, living or dead, actual events, locales or organizations is entirely coincidental. The publisher does not have any control over and does not assume any responsibility for author or third party websites or their content.

No part of this publication may be reproduced, stored in a retrieval system, or transmitted, in any form of binding or cover other than that in which it is published and without a similar condition being imposed on the subsequent purchaser.

For more information about SciFutures, go to: www.scifutures.com

Cover Illustration Copyright © 2016 Holly Heisey
Cover Design by Holly Heisey
Check out more of her work at: http://hollyheiseydesign.com

Formatting by Polgarus Studio

Contents

Foreword 1

Introduction 5

Learning to Speak Tiger - Trina Marie Phillips 9

Love in a Lonely City 2050 - Deborah Walker 29

Light Times - Ari Popper 43

Houseproud - Laurence Raphael Brothers 53

L.A. Loves You - Christopher Cornell 75

One Bad Apple - Holly Schofield 81

The Calculus of Trees - Sofie Bird 93

Chicago Blues - Gary Kloster 111

The Drowned City - Bo Balder 125

Foreword
The Mechanisms for Change

A few years ago I was in Stockholm Sweden on a book tour. It was snowing outside. I was on a small stage in a cramp room full of earnest journalists. After introductions, one of them asked "What will the future look like?"

I m used to these kinds of questions. Being a futurist, it's my job to work with organizations who need to make decisions and investments today that might not pay off for 10, 20 or even 30 years. It's my job to explore what it will feel like to live in the future.

"The future is going to look a lot like today," I answered.

Murmurs and skeptical laughs rumbled around the room. The journalists didn't like this answer. "How can that be?" another journalist pushed me to explain.

Humans don't like change. We don't want our cities to radically change. To prove my point, I noted that in Stockholm there were buildings that were older than America, my country.

They laughed.

It shouldn't surprise them, I continued, that things don't change all that quickly. People pay more money, oftentimes, for a house that's old than one that's brand new. As human beings we don't like change.

1

"Why would we want the world to transform in just a few short years?" I said.

They nodded and then another reporter asked me when the robots would take over the world -but that's a different story all together.

The Truth about the Future

The truth about the future is that the world really doesn't change that much, and humans don't really want it to change that much. We like things to stay the same. If you woke up one morning and walked out your front door and found the world had been completely transformed into a super space age landscape you'd freak out.

Don't get me wrong, things *do* change as we move into the future, but what changes and how it changes is typically quite subtle, even invisible. The appearance of the world around us may be radically transformed but the culture, economics and technology that lies beneath is constantly changing.

This is no more evident than in cities of the future.

Cities are important to people. We like cities. Humans started living in cities around 3000 BC in Mesopotamia, India, China, and Egypt give or take a few centuries. And we have never looked back. According to the United Nations, by the middle of 2009, the number of people living in urban areas (3.42 billion) had surpassed the number living in rural areas (3.41 billion).

Cities transform themselves slowly they have deep legacies both technological and cultural. For change to happen, it takes people and a shared vision.

How the Future Happens

"If you want to imagine cities of the future the thing to remember is that cities are for humans," Richard Sear explains. Richard is a Partner and Senior Vice President in the Visionary Innovation Group at the firm Frost and Sullivan. He works with mayors and city planners from some of the United States' largest cities. "All too often when people imagine future cities they think about the technology, but that's all wrong. Cities are for humans, not technology. By starting with a technology focus your solutions will be backwards at best."

The future isn't an accident. The future doesn't just happen. The future is built everyday by the actions of people. Organizations, governments, corporations and communities build the future. When a large group of people have an opinion about the future it matters, especially when it comes to cities.

"Cities will have to behave differently as well," Sear goes on to explain. "Cities will become like businesses."

But who wins and who loses in the city of tomorrow? There's a cautionary view that the decisions we make now could have deep impact on the future.

Jathan Sadowski is a politics of technology researcher at the School for the Future of Innovation in Society at Arizona State University. I am a professor of practice at the school and we have been talking about cities of the future. Jathan provides a needed voice of caution when thinking about the metropolises of tomorrow.

"Many smart city initiatives are based on systems of control and practices of *dataveillance*," he explains. "These powerful technologies have the potential to transform cities, but the question is, *Who will be doing the transforming and for whose benefit?* It is not yet clear that smart cities will contribute to ideals like social justice and human flourishing, rather than elite interests and value extraction."

How to Change the Future

When people have an opinion about the future, it matters. But there is something that matters more. There is a specific way that people can change the future.

How do you change the future? You change the story people tell themselves about the future they will live in. It's a simple thing but it can have massive effects. If you can change the story that people tell themselves about the future, then they will make different decisions. They will take different actions. They will bring about a very different tomorrow.

Cities and their futures are stories that we tell ourselves. We want to live in cities. We want to belong to communities. It's all the narrative we are telling ourselves and each other about the future we want to inhabit.

That's why this anthology is so important. You are holding in your hand a tool that can actually change the future. This collection of words and characters and visions is a future changing machine. Inside its pages is a multitude of possible futures that you can choose from. Be careful. Read with caution. Read with intent. You might actually be reading about your life and the lives of your children.

But to truly change the future you have to not only imagine it but you also have to have an opinion about it. You have to ask yourself what kind of future do you want to live in? What kind of future do you want to avoid? Then you have to talk to others about it.

Stories are mechanisms for change.

That's how you change the future. Have opinions and then talk about them with others.

It's that important. The future involves all of us. So get started!

Brian David Johnson

SciFutures Advisory Board Member
Futurist and Fellow – Frost and Sullivan
Futurist in Residence – Center for Science and the Imagination – Arizona State University

Introduction

I am in a unique position. First and foremost, I am a science fiction writer. As a science fiction writer, I'm trained to ask, "How can this go wrong?" That's the root of the story and the ensuing drama. It's how a smart house ends up kidnapping its family, and a spaceship AI murders the crew and locks its people out. From cautionary futuristic stories to hard sci-fi to space opera adventure, things going wrong makes for good story.

But as a futurist, I prefer to ask, "How can we make sure this goes right?" It doesn't always, even with the best of intentions, but that's what keeps stories interesting. I look for the positive spin because I believe the future we're headed for, while it's sure to be challenging, is going to be beneficial for the majority of humanity.

Science fiction and futurism: two sides of the same coin, but never a simple edge to walk. This is what I do every day, coming up with compelling narratives to help make sense of the future that is rushing toward us. We are living in a fantastic time, when technology is at a point where the future isn't going to happen to us, but we're going to shape how it happens. This is why science fiction stories are so inspiring and why we use them to illustrate the path forward for businesses, because if we can think it, we can make it happen.

At SciFutures, we work with over seventy science fiction writers that help us craft our narratives and ideate for our Fortune 500 clients. Often, our writers are asked to come up with scenarios for very specific needs, which can be a fun venture. But we also know that we have a trove of creative talent in our writing pool, and that's part of our purpose in creating this anthology, to let our writers spread their visionary wings. So we set them to work on ideas for the City of the Future set in the years 2020-2050.

Oh, the wonderful ideas they came up with.

This made choosing the final stories very difficult. It was a blind process. Every manuscript was stripped of the author's information. In this way, I could be completely impartial and select stories based entirely on merit. Since the staff at SciFutures was also able to submit, it guaranteed that I wouldn't feel pressure to choose a story based on job preservation or other considerations. In fact, the pressure shifted from *me* worrying, to our CEO, Ari Popper, feeling the pressure of wondering whether his story would make the final cut, (it did). That's the fear of rejection that every writer knows.

In the final selection we have romance and crime dramas, techno thrillers and adventure, in settings that span the global future from Iowa to Nigeria to London to Vietnam. There are stories that will make you laugh and some that will keep you on the edge of your seat. All of them will make you think.

As a last note, editors of anthologies don't usually include their own stories for the obvious lack of impartiality. However, being the Senior Writer at SciFutures, I wear many hats. And if you're reading this anthology because you want to see what we're all about, it seems to me that a sample of my writing should be present as well.

Now it's time to dive in. Brace yourself, the future is closer than you think.

Happy reading!

Trina Marie Phillips
Sr. Writer and Creative Futurist at SciFutures

Learning to Speak Tiger
Trina Marie Phillips

The monsoon raged overhead, pounding the heavy fortification tarps and creating a roar that had Nu convinced the city was under attack by a herd of elephants. At least, that's what she thought when she was younger. With the most subtle flourish, part of her trademark style, she put the finishing touches on the calligraphy of the message. In this day of holograms and bio-comm chips, the most honorable way to convey important information was to use a human to write and deliver it. That was her. She was only thirteen, but she wanted to be the best in Hanoi.

Nu had never been the best at anything. Her grades were average, and she never won any awards; her teachers had all but said she'd better find a good husband because she'd never excel beyond what a menial bot could do. They didn't understand. Sometimes she had to take her time, and be more careful in learning things, like calligraphy. After a lot of practice, Nu was as good as any of the older messengers. They could tease her about being slow because of her short legs, but they couldn't fault her penmanship.

But with this job, she might just show them all up. The recipient was the great business-master, Vinh Dong, and he was notorious for never sending human messengers; troi oi, he barely tolerated receiving them. If Nu could convince him otherwise...

Though it was probably just a tall dream. Vinh Dong was the most important businessman in the country. To him, no one was worthy enough for him to send a human messenger. Asked how he communicated with Vietnam's president, he said, "I do not waste her time by foregoing technology."

Nu finished her last swallow of tea. Before the fill-bot could replenish her cup, she gestured her cut off point. She double- and triple-checked her work against the original message on her wrist holo, then rolled the paper and slid it into the bronze transport cylinder. Upon sealing it, the sender would receive word and could track her progress through the city. Everyone, even the poorest people, had census chips implanted somewhere on their body. Nu's family wasn't radically poor, but every little bit eased her parent's stress. So when this work experience opportunity came around for school credit, she jumped on it.

The transport cylinder slid easily into the pocket of her red silk tunic. The traditional style of her uniform belied the wearable technology embedded in the beautiful dragon fabric that monitored her physical status, reminding her to hydrate if she ran for a long time or to stop and eat if her glucose levels fell too low. With a wink at the fill-bot, Nu closed her modest tab at the tea house and took off.

Undaunted by the rain that would never reach her, she weaved her way through the packed streets of the Old Quarter; the warm light from the tarps, created by the kinetic energy of the rain, lighting her path. Nu dodged around an older woman walking with a cane. She could hear the servos in the woman's hip working, a recent surgery if she still needed the cane assist. Then Nu slid into the street, keeping pace in her run with a bicycle laden front to back with huge bundles of fresh flowers. An old transport method, but surely every blossom was micro-tagged for inventory.

Scoots owned the center of the road with only a few intrepid car drivers to be found braving the streets. Every year the automakers claimed to make their cars the smartest ever, but the controlled human chaos of the Old Quarter defeated the auto-drives every time. The locals owned the streets, and they knew it; they weren't going to let some robot tell them where to walk.

The smell of spicy grilled fish and vegetables from a street vendor wafted across Nu's path outdoing the aroma of the cut blooms she ran alongside. She smiled privately at the thriving pulse of her neighborhood.

Nu cut across the street. A bright orange scoot rolled straight toward her. Nu danced out of the way, receiving a honk from the driver. Not so slow as those older kids would have her believe, she chuckled. These were her streets. No way some silly scoot driver would tag her.

It wasn't long before the Old Quarter gave way to the more orderly nature of Greater Hanoi. Street displays showed clearly the path for cars, the one for scoots and the space for pedestrians. Almost no one drove. Riders focused on their holo-displays, getting work done, or shopping, letting the cars handle transport. The pitch of the rain vibrating on the tarps lowered as they stretched across wider streets; and these not only lit up, but played animations of dragons flying through the clouds. The tarps didn't cover every street in the city, but Nu had planned her route for minimal wetness.

As she approached the corner stop, Nu called out the bus she was hoping for. The holo-sign at the stop lit with its route and exact location. Two minutes out. Sometimes it was easier to run, but two minutes? She could wait.

Bus-luck was with her and Nu made her transfers smoothly. But now she was uptown and there was a conspicuous lack of tarps protecting the streets. People walked, unbothered by the downpour. These were the richest of the rich, and their personal weather shields separated them from the workers and service people who scurried with their rain hats, or under umbrellas. The shields were thumb-sized devices worn on lapels or collars. They used the kinetic energy of the storm to control the movement of molecules around the user, creating a perfectly comfortable environment; and they cost more than most people made in a year.

Nu pulled out the collapsible hat she carried from the deep pocket in her pants. The yellow cube looked unimpressive in her palm until she twisted a corner and the walls uncoiled in sequence, converting it into a traditional non la hat. It was a modified conical design that she'd programmed on an old 3D printer. Simple, but functional, it was better than most umbrellas.

Relying on the city AI to anticipate her path and keep the autonomous vehicles out of her way, Nu made her dash for Vitality Tower, the kilometer-high center of Vinh Dong's empire. Most of the building was made of solar cell glass and transparent aluminum honeycomb, giving the distorted illusion of being able to see into the building while actually showing nothing. Today the rain spotted surface faceted the image further, reflecting the grey of the sky and the darkest grey of the street making the tower look like it was sprinkled with pepper. The building materials were a point of pride for Dong, and for Vietnam. Manufactured locally, they were the cornerstone of Dong's success.

Nu bypassed the slidewalk into the lobby and sped by on foot. The circuit in the message tube communicated her authorized presence to security, and the hotel AI; the floor lit up in front of her, guiding her to her destination. She dashed for the elevator, collapsed her hat and checked her reflection on the inside of the elevator door to make sure her tidiness met professional messenger standards. Nu flattened a few stray hairs and straightened herself. The translucent elevator slid up, and to the left; there was a pause before the car shifted to a gold-tinged shaft. The number display disappeared, with only one word remaining: Summit. Nu's stomach tingled.

The summit was not filled with the busy chaos she expected. The lobby was dark and cool with plush crimson carpet and the walls tinted to a dark smoky transparency. The large open space was empty of furniture, and people; the only thing that filled it was eerie silence and the bipedal robot that stood by a single door on the far side of the room.

Nanofibers in the carpet still glowed, directing her. When she didn't move immediately, the signal pulsed with gentle urgency. No, she didn't want to dawdle, or appear to be late. Now was the time. Nu took a deep breath and strode forward.

The robot acknowledged her and opened the door without Nu having to break her stride. Inside Vinh Dong's office the carpet continued, but the walls were morphed to let in far more light, almost achingly so after the dark of the anteroom. Nu paused to let her eyes adjust. When her vision cleared, she saw Vinh Dong, from the back, as he finished a holovid call. He was neither tall nor short, and on the street he would not stand out in any way. The office looked like it was designed by a professional, giving nothing of Dong himself away, except for the holopics of his family, a wife and three kids, that floated here and there.

Then the man turned and in that simple gesture, Nu sensed his power. Pure confidence in his bearing. Feeling the insignificance of her position as a lowly messenger from the Old Quarter, Nu instinctively wanted to bow, or kneel, or turn and run. She wasn't important enough to be here. But her mother had taught her different. She said that no person was greater than any other. That she should always hold her head high. So that's what she did, though she couldn't stop her insides from shaking.

Nu stepped forward, and using two hands, presented the message cylinder to Vinh Dong. The businessman took the cylinder with one hand, impassive, appraising.

"Mr. Dong, I bring you greetings from Mr. Bao Phan," Nu said.

Dong read the message in a glance and the right side of his lip sneered. "You bring me excuses and half-truths, young lady."

Her mother had also told her never to apologize for wrongs that weren't hers. "That may be so. You will have to take that up with Mr. Phan. Would you like to send a return message? I do not mind writing impolite things."

Dong chuckled. "No. There will be no response." He handed the cylinder back to Nu and floated the message into the path of a hidden recycler beam on the corner of his desk that instantly dismantled the paper and sucked the particles away.

He started to turn away, dismissing her. Nu froze. Any opportunity she had to change his mind, or make an impression, was slipping away. This would be her only chance. Maybe she was crazy, or maybe she was as dull as everyone thought, but she quickly slid the cylinder into its carry pocket and pulled out one of her personal business cards.

"Mr. Dong."

He paused, barely turning his head back toward her.

Nu squared her shoulders. "Mr. Dong, I would like to present you with my card, should you require my services in the future." She held her card out with two hands. The ink gif activated immediately and the image of an antelope bounded gracefully across the top of the card and off the edge, before repeating.

Vinh Dong turned fully, surprising her. Nu braced for a verbal assault, but his response was calm.

"You know my reputation?" he asked.

"Yes."

"And yet you offer me this?"

"One day, there may be someone important enough for you to need me," Nu said, proud that she'd kept the waver out of her voice.

Dong took the card, again with one hand, and watched the animation. "Not bad, for one so young. But I build my world on greatness, not adequacy." And with a flick of his wrist, her card flew into the beam, disintegrated, and was sucked away.

Nu couldn't hide her disappointment, but she didn't think he saw anything because he had already turned away. She had been dismissed.

That night, Nu pondered greatness. The concept seemed so far away. Then again, most of her classmates didn't even have their own business cards, much less ones so elegant. But this was the real world; she couldn't measure herself alongside other children and expect to measure up. In fact, she was thirteen. If she was ever going to be anything, she needed to stop thinking of herself as a dull child, or even a child at all. She had designed and programmed that card herself. There was no reason she couldn't compete on the adult playing field, right? She just needed to figure out what would impress Mr. Dong.

The goal was to get him to accept her business card, which made the next level obvious; she had to jump from two dimensions to three. That meant learning the advanced program language. Nu wouldn't be eligible to take the class in school for another two years, but she could find free instruction in the stream, she was sure of it.

Three weeks went by and after school, and her messenger job, she spent the remainder of her time working her new skill. The program, which was actually a series of finely scored lines in programmable, paper-thin nanometal, was getting very complex and took up the front and back of the card; and still it wasn't right. She'd been through many attempts. Fortunately, the material took to sanding about three times before it became unusable. Unfortunately, the little extra money she kept from her paycheck for herself had turned into a pile of discarded nanometal.

It was another week before she perfected her new card. She kept the antelope motif but instead of ink moving across the card, it now folded itself into an origami antelope that bounded across the table. Left to its programming, it would run in a circle, but Nu could use gesture commands to change its path, to keep it from running off of Mr. Dong's desk, or avoid obstacles.

She was so proud when she got it to work that she did a little dance in her room.

The matter of hacking the original message tube with a new date stamp so she would be able to return to the summit without being stopped by security turned out to be simple, compared to what she had just accomplished. Of course, if she got caught, it would mean the end of her career as a messenger. The risk weighed heavy on her. If she never tried, she'd never know if she could be great. But losing her job would be a burden to her family.

After a long internal debate, Nu set the delivery time on the message tube for the next day. Failure would cost, but she had a chance at greatness for once in her life; she'd never forgive herself if she didn't try.

***

The city was still damp from the morning's storm, but the rains were in their final throes of the season which left a break, an afternoon of sunshine. Nu chose the high route through mid-town so she could walk along the elevated parkway to help focus her mind. Only pedestrians and small-wheeled vehicles were allowed amidst the grassy areas and dense green landscaping, nothing that hovered or flew. Wide paved spaces made room for people to meet, or exercise, or dance. A handful of approved vendors made food and drink available and there were plenty of places to sit and enjoy the escape from the hectic city below. Nu had heard that Singapore had a similar park, but theirs ran the entire length of the island and had bright yellow trolley cars. She'd like to see that one day, maybe on a business trip, if she ever became successful.

Nu's pace was brisker than most here, but that didn't mean she wasn't enjoying the scenery. All of the buildings near the parkway had long ago had their facades covered in living concrete so even the surrounding architecture looked like a continuation of the park landscape. The plants on the buildings did all sorts of good things for the environment; they cleaned the air, made good use of water, and acted as natural insulation. That was one of the first things they learned in school, how important the environment was.

From here, Nu could see the solar panels or gardens that lined every rooftop; wind farms and water reclamation were used everywhere. It was an international obsession. Even the monsoon tarps guided the rain water into great collection chambers so it could be distributed to areas suffering from drought. Nu's parents were always a little bitter about the damage from previous generations that they had to clean up. Nu and her friends saw the environmental problem on the mend and weren't so upset. But knowing what could have been, she understood why the lessons of the past were so important.

The descent down to street level was a shock she'd grown used to. Cars, buses, scoots and bicycles, though orderly, still felt like chaos as compared to above. Nu felt good, relaxed and refreshed, so she dashed the few remaining blocks to uptown. They didn't need an elevated park. Almost every building there had an oasis to escape to.

There was no pepper effect on Vitality Tower today. It was clear and bright but, as designed, not blindingly so. Nu paused as a surge of doubt assaulted her mind. Was she risking too much? She was breaking rules and violating the wishes of Vinh Dong himself. This really wasn't a very smart idea.

No, she had to believe she could do this. She wondered how her parents would take the news if she got caught. Dad would be angry; Mom would be…proud that she tried…maybe, hopefully. The imagined glimmer of support helped set her mind.

Nu stepped into Vitality Tower. The hack on the cylinder worked and the indicators in the carpet showed her the path she already knew. With every breath on the way to the summit, she tried to breathe in confidence and breathe out worry. She would never be successful if she couldn't banish doubt.

When the elevator doors opened, the space looked very different than the last time she'd been here. It still had the same dark carpet, but the room was bright, set up with polished diamond high tables and carved teak chairs. New nano-patterned partitions, obviously morphed from the original wall, broke the space into smaller meeting nooks. Still no people. Nu wondered what a meeting of people worthy enough to come to the summit would look like. They would have to be the greatest of the great. She would love to see that, to be in a room with all those brilliant minds.

Nu couldn't see all the way across the room, but the indicators in the carpet guided her around the new configuration until she stood in front of Vinh Dong's office once again. She didn't allow herself but a breath to hesitate before she marched into Dong's office. Vinh Dong sat behind his desk, slouched, chin in his hand, staring out into space. He didn't seem to notice her entrance, or if he did, he was ignoring her. Nu was surprised. She never expected to see this man looking so…human. It was then she realized that he wasn't staring into space, but at a hologram of his children.

"What is it?" The gravity of a black hole pulled on Vinh Dong's words, combined with a satellite of annoyance. This was the worst time Nu could possibly have chosen for her presentation, but there was no going back.

"Mr Dong, I would like to present you with my card." Nu held the card out with both hands, only momentarily, until she was sure she had his attention. Then she set it on the desk before she started shaking, and flicked her little finger, the gesture for it to begin folding.

The card worked perfectly. After a few seconds of folding, the antelope began its run. A stylus lay in its path so Nu gestured with a middle finger flick and the antelope leapt over the stylus. With a tap on the table, she made the spontaneous program change to permanent so it jumped the stylus on every lap. She was proud. She didn't dance, or celebrate outwardly, but she knew her eyes must be shining from the change in Dong's expression. His face went from doubt, to curious. Except all of his curiosity fell on her. His lapse to human disappeared and his sharp gaze met her eyes. The look was designed to make people flinch; she almost did, but when she recognized this, something inside of her refused to do so.

"I remember you." He glanced at the antelope running around on his desk.

Dong stood, walked around his desk and leaned against it with his arms crossed, looking sideways at her. "Are you counting on my kindness not to call security?"

Nu gasped slightly and her chest tightened. She had talked herself into believing that this wouldn't happen. It's not like she was a real threat. Ah, but he saw her as a pest.

Or did he?

Dong hadn't called security yet, which he could've done the moment she stepped into his office with no message to deliver. She

19

still had an opening, if she didn't hesitate. She was in too deep to not take a chance now. Nu squelched her fear and stepped back so she could look him more directly in the eye.

"I'm counting on your respect."

Dong tilted his head and his cheek muscle twitched. He was amused.

Dong pushed off the desk and rose, facing her squarely. Without looking, he pointed at the running antelope.

"Is this your best?" was all he said.

Nu's eyes followed his finger and she watched her creation running around in that simple circle, jumping the stylus repeatedly. Her glance slid around the desk with its accessories made of platinum and diamond, and a hologram of Dong and his kids in front of his ultra-modern mansion. Then she looked back to her antelope and knew; she had not achieved greatness.

Nu dipped her head slightly. "No. It is not."

Dong reached over and made a counter-clockwise swirling motion with his finger, uncoiling the antelope's path. With another flick, he redirected Nu's creation into the recycler beam at the corner of his desk. Phhht, and its remains were sucked away.

Nu took a deep breath and let it out intently. Disappointment in herself gnawing at her gut. Failure didn't sit well, especially when it was her own fault.

"Look inside, young one, and I think you'll find that you are not an antelope, you are not prey."

Surprised, Nu looked up at Vinh Dong. His eyes were patient, knowing. He was giving her another chance. She knew it would be her last.

***

Nu made her way to the Temple of Literature. She wouldn't call herself a Confucianist, but she liked the calm, orderliness of the temple with its simple pagoda-style roofs. In the third courtyard in particular was one of her favorite thinking spots, the Well of Heavenly Clarity, a large rectangular pool surrounded by carved stone walls. She leaned on one of two low, ironwork gates, staring into the green water. Clarity was something she desperately needed. All that work that she'd been so proud of, and it wasn't enough. Of course it wasn't. The running antelope was her first success. She had mistaken her feeling of accomplishment for greatness. They were nowhere near the same thing. But what was greatness made of? How would she know when she achieved it?

And then there was what Vinh Dong had said, that she wasn't prey. He obviously believed in her on some level, but she didn't feel like a predator. She didn't know what she was supposed to be. Maybe she was wrong about being ready to compete with adults. Maybe this was all too much for her. But even as she thought it, her mind rebelled against the negativity.

From behind her, the gentle whir of a robotic monk approached. The bot rolled up alongside of her and paused. Its matte crimson shell was a minimalist design looking like a thick, round-cornered post with an angle-cut top where the screen with its glowing blue eyes served as an interface.

"Is there something you would like assistance reflecting on?" the monk-bot asked. Nu realized that it was interacting with the biometrics in her uniform and sensed her distress.

Nu looked at the bot and considered whether it would be able to help. "Okay, how do you know when you've achieved greatness?"

"Have you ever achieved greatness before?" the bot asked.

That made Nu think. Occasionally she'd done well on school projects and tests; and there were times when she accomplished something that she thought was special, even if no one else did, but the reality was all too obvious.

"No," Nu answered.

The bot launched into a tourist-level Confucianism lecture about the path to align with heavenly attributes and lost her interest entirely. The monk-bot was merely for show.

"Never mind," she said. "Leave me."

The robot fell into silence, turned and rolled away.

Nu stayed and stared into the water until she got pinged on her wrist-holo. The house AI knew how far away she was and was telling her when Dad would be done cooking dinner. The sun was mostly down; she'd have to leave soon. Nu searched for clarity for another minute, then two. She had one more chance with Vinh Dong, but no idea what to do with it.

After dinner, Nu kept to herself. Not that she hadn't been doing that with the card project, but not actually working on something and staring off in deep thought drew her mother's attention. Mom sat next to her on the couch.

"Something heavy is on your mind. Share with me," Mom said.

Nu sighed, but after a moment's hesitation she started to tell her Mom about that afternoon, and ended up telling her everything about her encounters with Vinh Dong.

"So you trespassed to present him with your second card?" In that moment, Mom's eyes became hard, assessing. "That was quite a risk."

Nu stopped breathing under her mother's gaze, waiting for the scolding. But Mom's shoulders relaxed and her expression softened.

"He's right. You are not prey," Mom said. "You are bold, like me. Don't fear it."

"But I don't know what he wants."

"I think the question is, what do you want?"

"I want to be great, but I don't know how. I don't know who I am, or what I want. How can I be a predator if I don't know myself?"

Nu heard the whine in her voice and regretted it. She was trying not to act like a child.

"That's very insightful." Mom folded her hands in quiet contemplation and paused a long while before finally speaking. "Maybe you shouldn't be asking yourself who you are, but who it is you want to be."

Nu started to give a response, but realized she didn't have one. That was a question she could answer. Not right this minute, but given time, this answer was within her grasp. Her Mom had a patient expression, not unlike Vinh Dong's had been that afternoon. The adults weren't going to hand her the answer. They'd rather watch her suffer. No. This was something they couldn't answer for her. She shook her head.

"Come on," Mom said, "the best place to start looking for revelation is in a bowl of ice cream."

Nu laughed. "Really? What great philosopher said that?"

Mom shrugged, "I did. Besides, I'm sure Sakyamuni himself would have agreed, if they'd had refrigeration at the time."

Nu let her Mom pull her to her feet and drag her into the kitchen. She was right. The bottom of a scoop of cinnamon ice cream was a great place to start looking for clarity.

***

The summit had changed appearance again. There were still plenty of diamond-topped tables, now covered with platters of modern Vietnamese dim sum, but fewer partitions and lots of people. All well-dressed, Nu recognized some of the business leaders and scientists and thought-leaders of the day, but even those she didn't had a sense of bearing, and belonging. They gathered in clumps and talked, discussing graphs and formulas brought up on competing holo-displays. This was the meeting of minds she had only imagined, and she was amazed that even with the hacked message tube that the automated security system let her up here. Nu's world felt suddenly small.

She didn't see any chance that she'd be able to get a private moment with Vinh Dong, if any moment at all. But just being here, with all of these brilliant people, even if only for a few minutes, felt like a privilege.

The indicator in the rug pulsed and guided Nu across the room. She hoped she had gotten her card right this time. More weeks, more nanometal and blades than she could count. And then there was the final card made out of the special reflective material. She'd had to save for two weeks just to buy a single piece, and the nerves she'd spent scoring it caused more stress than a year's worth of exams all on one day.

Of the important people in the room, several took notice of her. With everyone knowing Vinh Dong's attitude toward messengers, she had to be a strange sight. They watched with curiosity, and a few looks of pity. But she knew something they didn't. She was welcome here, at least for her last attempt to impress. That realization flipped Nu's mind a little. On one level, she was equal to all of the amazing people in this room.

In practice, her card's success rate was as good as any of the manned space programs out there; and at that, she had to say good enough. This time she was truly proud of what she'd accomplished. She hadn't just made a technical accomplishment, but, she felt, a conceptual one as well. Graceful, but strong; complex, yet simple.

Nu didn't hesitate entering Vinh Dong's office. She might succeed, or she might fail here, but as she crossed the room she became more and more certain of who she wanted to be. Vinh Dong was speaking to a small group of people on the far side of his desk. Nu waited patiently for her presence to draw his attention. When it did, the tiniest smile cracked the corner of his mouth.

"So, you return," Vinh Dong said. He turned in a way that drew the crowd of people nearest him to pay attention to her as well. Such command, with the slightest body language. Nu would have to learn that. She nodded to him.

"Mr. Dong, I would like to present you with my card." She held it out like she had before. Dong took a step toward her, the crowd followed with a collective gasp at the messenger that had such audacity.

Nu set the card on the desk, glanced up at Dong, and set it into motion. Once again, the card folded itself into an origami antelope and started running in a circle. Some of the crowd was impressed; no doubt taking her age into consideration. Vinh Dong looked at her, not fooled. He knew she had more tricks in her bag. Nu reached over, making the same gesture Dong had, unwinding the path and sending the antelope straight for the recycler beam. Dong gasped, ever so slightly.

The antelope leapt through the beam. The reflective coating turned a deep bronze color, but did not disintegrate. And as the beam struck it, the antelope transformed, not refolding, but reshaping the planes of its surface until it finished the leap in the form of a tiger. Nu squealed inside; having only a single sheet, she had been unable to test the material's reaction to the beam. Outwardly though, she remained calm.

A slight gesture from Nu kept the tiger from running off the edge of the desk. With a finger flick, she made the tiger run toward center desk, and toward Vinh Dong. The tiger came to a skidding stop and let out a tinny roar. The surface planes shifted again until the tiger had transformed into the figure of a hooded young woman. When the figure finished forming, it looked up, and the hood fell back to reveal a holographic projection of Nu's face. The crowd gasped, and then clapped, delighted.

Even Vinh Dong was smiling openly. He stepped around the desk and put his hand on her shoulder.

"Well done. You understand, now," he said.

Nu nodded. "I do."

"Then I have a task for you."

Vinh Dong led her to the balcony. The city stretched out below them, the new and the old, flowing through and around each other in an intricate dance that was distinctly Hanoi. But Vinh Dong's demeanor had changed. He was not the party host out here. Something weightier was on his mind.

"You have learned what it takes to be successful. Now I'm going to tell you something far more important in the hope that you don't have to learn it the hard way."

Nu looked at him questioningly. All that work she did, and something else was more important?

Dong continued. "No matter how much you do, or what you have, it's the people around you that make you rich."

It only took a moment for Nu to think about how it was her Mom's suggestion that led her on the path to her success; and the constant support she always had from her family.

"Whatever you do, don't neglect them."

Nu nodded, knowing from his tone that he was speaking from personal experience. "I understand," she said gently.

"I want you to deliver a message to my wife. Tell her I'm ready to step away from the business to be with her and the kids."

Nu was shocked. The biggest business man in Vietnam was going to walk away? She pointed back toward the room full of people.

"Do they know?"

Dong shook his head. "I need to know if she'll take me back."

Nu couldn't believe she was the only person with this news. She didn't have to be told that discretion was required here. Nu pulled up her holo display and started taking down his words like she would with any message delivery. Vinh Dong put his hand over her wrist, stopping her.

"I like that you speak with an honest heart. Tien will recognize that. Tell her with your voice."

"I would be honored," Nu said.

"She's at our villa outside of the city. The Skyline should have you there and home by dinner."

"The Skyline? Really?" Another first she never imagined. The Skyline was a luxury hovercar service that flew above the buildings but below the airplanes. To prevent congestion, only a certain number of flights were allowed each day.

Vinh Dong gave a little shrug. "You deserve it."

***

The Skyline server bot handed Nu the pale strawberry soda in a flute as if it were the finest pink champagne, and even toasted with her as they flew over the city. Vinh Dong's message was more than safe with her; she could now claim that she was the best messenger in Hanoi. But that accomplishment seemed small next to all she had learned. Nu understood now that the city was full of opportunity if she was bold enough to seize it. She could shape her future much like she had shaped that business card.

This was only the beginning.

Trina Marie Phillips is the Senior Writer and a Creative Futurist at SciFutures. Her work has appeared in Orson Scott Card's *Intergalactic Medicine Show* and *AE: The Canadian Science Fiction*

Review. She has attended the Science Fiction Master Class *Taos Toolbox* and been a Finalist for the *James White Award* and in the *Writers of the Future* contest. Trina is also a member of the Codex Writers Group and an Associate Member of SFWA.

LinkedIn: Trina Phillips
Facebook: https://www.facebook.com/trinamarie.phillips
Twitter: @TrinaMPhillips

Love in a Lonely City 2050
Deborah Walker

London might be a very smart city, but it can't stop the rain falling from August skies.

I could have asked the street to set a roving umbro around me and let the electrostatic field shield me, like most sensible people were doing. But I was *not* in a good mood. I wanted to get soaked. Let the rain ruin my fancy hair-do. Let the rain wash my mascara into streaks. I didn't care.

I stomped through Bloomsbury, rain tears running off the purple skin of my smart suede boots.

In a city of eleven million you'd think I'd be able to find a decent date.

"You're too picky," said my sister.

"You're just biding your time," said my father.

"You're just enjoying playing the field," said Sal, my recently divorced best friend who was having the time of her life, or so she claimed.

I linked into the local net, and streamed a live performance of *La Traviata* from the Syrian Opera Players. Love, death and divas: the opera suited my mood. I skirted around a flock of young girls taking up half the street while coordinating their hydro-perox jetpacks. They shot into the air in a cloud of water-vapour, heading to a sky-high café where they'd while away the afternoon with good coffee and better gossip.

The rain! The incessant rain! In August! Still, it was good for the living walls and the green roofs. But not so good for the photovoltaic panels on almost every building. We hadn't had much sun this month, perhaps my home building wouldn't show an energy surplus. The thought that I might actually have to pay an energy bill in summer sent my mood plummeting. And I thought I'd plumbed the depths of despair after the terrible, terrible date I'd just escaped from.

So much for Love A.I. So much for its wild claims of perfect compatibility. I ought to ask for my money back. Maybe try the old-fashioned route next time and avoid technology altogether. Most of my friends felt a compulsion to fix me up all the time. They thought it was a little bit sad that I was thirty-five and had never been in a relationship that lasted more than six months. But hey, it's 2050. A woman can be perfectly happy without a man.

Except that I wasn't. I was lonely. Woman cannot live by work alone, at least not this woman.

Which is why I'd succumbed to the lure of the perfect blind date. Oh, we were eminently compatible according to Love A.I. We'd met in the park for a picnic. We were both Londoners, so we should have known better than to fix an outdoor date in August, especially in a green belt field without umbro shields.

The date had been a tense hour of looking up at the darkening sky. The salient feature of the date was the lack of conversation. Oh sure, there was talking: quite a lot of it, as I babbled on. I have a tendency to babble when I'm nervous, and nothing makes me more nervous than a man frowning at the overcast sky and not saying much at all: an interesting man, a surgeon at Great Ormond Street, a 92%

compatible man who apparently had nothing to say for himself. Perhaps it was me. Perhaps I'd made him nervous with my ultra-babble. When I felt the first drops of rain, I'd made my apologies and a quick getaway. No harm, no foul. Nobody's fault, just another mismatched romantic non-experience. I was beginning to think that there was no one around for me. Perhaps all the good men were taken. But in a city of eleven million there were a *lot* of single men. Except I'd been dating for a long time. It was all beginning to look rather hopeless.

No more blind dates, I told myself, splashing through the puddles pooling on the green recycled concrete of Russel Square. Overhead, gigantic balloons filled with hydrogen producing algae bobbed gently in the fierce rain. A workman was siphoning off the hydrogen to stationary fuel cells which would convert the hydrogen into liquid fuel.

"Nice day for ducks," he said.

"If you like that sort of thing," I replied, noticing he was rather attractive, and rather wet. I liked a man who didn't mind getting wet. Wouldn't it be funny if I met someone as I was escaping from the dating disaster? Discreetly I sent a query to his personal comm to check his status. He was married. He had three beautiful children. Just my luck.

At least you could discreetly and *anonymously* check people out nowadays. As long as they had their profiles public. That was a big time saver. I walked quickly on.

There are eighty million people in England. A goodly number of them must have been single men looking for the love of a good woman. Perhaps I should cast my net beyond the lonely city. Nip up to Birmingham, Manchester, Leeds— anywhere on the High Speed Trainet. Anywhere. I was aware that I was beginning to sound slightly desperate. And that is not an attractive quality in man or woman.

I was heading to Senate House where I socio-volunteered as a rare book librarian. Even through it was Saturday, I might as well get a couple of hours work in. No sense letting the day be a total washout.

Multi-use Senate House was buzzing, as usual. As well as being the University of London's library it was currently housing three funky pop-up cafes, an experimental art-food-human rights installation, a couple of open welfare support groups and the peripatetic civil service was utilising any excess space. I stood outside for a few moments, mulling over my options. Was it me or was just everyone in London coupled up and loving it? A crocodile of a dozen men walked past, each paired off, holding hands, looking blissfully happy, probably some university club outing. I should really put in a few hours at the library. But . . . But . . . I wasn't in the mood. I didn't know what I *was* in the mood for. "What do you think I should do?" I asked the lamppost.

The lamppost linked to my data-preferences in my personal comm, and suggested two local cafes that sold my favourite brew and suggested a route to each of them.

I'm not in the mood for coffee, I subvocalised. Shocking words, I know. That tells you what type of foul mood I was in.

The lamppost informed me there was a new exhibit at the British Museum.

I eye-flicked for more information. And then laughed aloud. The British Museum was doing Romance? Ha! Somehow that suited my twisted sense of humour.

The BM was just a hop, skip and a jump from Senate House, through the Botanical Vertical Gardens. This part of Bloomsbury has been pedestrianized for donkey's years, so, for once, I didn't have to dodge the irritating electric Boris Bikes that swarmed through most London streets.

***

The British Museum Great Court always takes my breath away. The massive glass dome was being particularly spectacular, back lit with storm clouds and pattering with rain. I stood for a few minutes silently greeting an old friend, the stone lion with his face hollowed by time and mournful. *You and me both, my friend.* But womanfully I made my way to the Romance temporary exhibit.

A gaggle of squealing children emerged from the Egyptian Galleries, wearing face masks. The museum was coming alive for them, perhaps they were being chased by Mummies or by wolf headed Anubis threatening to psychopomp them to the afterworld. Kids love things like that. The British Museum is no place of old-fashioned museum hush. It's easy enough for any visitor to ask the museum to filter out any annoying ambient noise. Kids can run about shouting their heads off. With noise filters they didn't have to disturb anyone.

The line for Romance was long, so I used the social credits I'd earned volunteering as a librarian to buy myself a fast-track.

I was greeted at the entrance by a hunky 18th century avatar, something of a dandy, tall, dark skinned and handsome with his long hair powdered, scented with cloves and exquisitely curled.

"Welcome, gentle lady. I am the Chevalier de Seingalt."

"Hello."

A small frown creased the avatar's high forehead. "Perhaps you know me by the name Giacomo Girolamo Casanova, citizen of the pleasure capital of the world, the fair Republic of Venice, renowned place of carnival, gambling houses, and beautiful courtesans?"

"Ah. Casanova. Of course you are. Hello."

"I am gratified that a small measure of my fame has reached your notice, señorita. And you too are a lover of books, I see." The avatar had accessed my public profile, tailoring its interactions to ensure that it wasn't being offensive to my cultural preferences. It was almost like having a conversation with a real person. In fact, better than a conversation with some people: ahem, mentioning no names: Mr Silent Doctor.

Casanova grinned. He looked me up and down, without any attempt at subtlety. Then he nodded in approval. I'm sad to say this was the closest I'd got to any 'man' showing interest in me for about a year. Casanova stepped closer to me. He said in a soft voice, "My library of forbidden books gives me great pleasure, perhaps we should discuss it?"

"I think I'll go into the exhibit, if you don't mind."

"But of course, my deepest apologies for making such an unwelcome suggestion, on this the day of love."

"No problem."

"A favour, dear lady," said Casanova sweeping his hand down low in a flourishing bow. "The creators of this pleasure experience would greatly appreciate your participation in a small experiment. They ask only your time for a quarter of the hour."

"Sure." I'd taken part in these experiments before. The creators, the curator, liked to test the efficiency of their avatars. Any feedback I gave would help the curators tailor their interactives to their users.

"Many thanks gracious lady, and may today be the day you find love."

"Ha!" I said striding into the museum.

The first room was low lit, and red. Couples strolled around happily amongst the expressions of love rendered in stone and metal and paint from thousands of years and from across the globe. As a world class museum, the British Museum had a lot of stuff to choose from, and they'd probably borrowed a few bits and pieces from other museums and galleries, too.

One man, all on his own caught my eye. He was singing. Actually singing. He was standing in front of Rossetti's painting *My Lady Greensleeves*, and singing—in an act of stunning originality—Greensleeves.

Alas, my love, you do me wrong,
To cast me off discourteously.
For I have loved you well and long,
Delighting in your company.

Greensleeves was all my joy
Greensleeves was my delight,
Greensleeves was my heart of gold,
And who but my lady greensleeves.

Alas, my love, that you should own
A heart of wanton vanity,
So must I meditate alone
Upon your insincerity.

Good grief. He was singing away without a care in the world. Who did he think he was? A troubadour or something? He certainly had an old fashioned look about him. Blonde shoulder length hair framed a square face. He was dressed rather damply. I guess he'd been caught out in the rain, too. It wasn't that he had a bad voice. He had a very fine voice, actually, but I can't stand those people who feel the need to sing in public. You find them on the London Lev, singing away, so sure of themselves, so arrogant.

He wasn't even singing that loudly. I could have asked the room to adjust the ambient incoming noise, but, as I might have mentioned, I was *very* a bad mood.

I stomped over to him. He stopped singing and looked a tad startled.

"Do you mind?" I said.

"Mind what?"

"You're singing. It's disturbing me."

He blushed. For a moment, I felt bad, but then I reminded myself that it was him, not me, who was in the wrong.

"Sure," he said. "But you could have just altered the noise level."

"I shouldn't have to." Anyway, I didn't want to get into a whole *thing* about it. "Thank you very much," I said, and stalked off.

***

The second room was bit sciency, looking at the biological base of love. Love as the mammalian drive as natural as hunger or thirst. This part of the exhibit seemed to be popular with men on their own. I saw them nodding seriously and looking intently at ancient flasks and test tubes.

One exhibit told me that love was an evolutionary trait designed to get a man and woman together long enough to propagate the continuation of the species. Especially as human kiddiewinks are about the most helpless creatures in the world, needing parental protection for a larger portion of their lifespans than any other mammals. Love then was the mechanism that kept parents together long enough to ensure that the kids grew up to have children of their own.

The psychology display explored the triangular theory of love as a cognitive and social phenomenon. I didn't really understand that, so I moved on to the wall panels discussing the three overlapping stages: lust, attraction, and attachment. I admired an artist's interpretation of three stages: the neural circuitry rendered in bronze tubes with opal neurotransmitters whizzling around the maze, and hormones lighting pathways of pulsing lights. That was love, was it?

Perhaps my neurotransmitters needed a little rebalancing. I activated the avatar of the famous love doctor, scientist and 30's media sensation: Aahva Poorelli:

"Is there a pill I can take to make someone fall in love with me?" I asked. I was only half-joking

"Alas no," said Dr Poorelli. "Although we can investigate the chemical basis of emotions, we're a long way from manipulating them." He smiled. "I guess we shouldn't. Where would be the fun in that?"

"I think you're right, Doctor. Loneliness can't be cured with a pill."

When someone tapped me on the shoulder, I nearly jumped out of my skin. That man, Greensleeves, had snuck up behind me.

"What?" I kinda snarled at him.

"You're speaking aloud, it's putting me off the enjoyment of the exhibit."

This time it was my turn to blush. Had he heard what I'd said? And if quiet conversation bothered him, he should have activated his noise filters.

"Oh, pardon me for breathing," I said.

"Apology accepted."

How childish! *Obviously,* I hadn't been disturbing him. He was only doing it to get payback for my earlier entirely responsible request for him to stop singing. I would have said something witty and cutting in reply, but Greensleeves wandered off before I had time to think of the *mot juste*.

Well, I wasn't going to let him spoil my enjoyment of the exhibition.

I left the science rooms. Let's face it: love was a phenomenon that defied quantification, otherwise the Love A.I. wouldn't have fixed me up with Doctor No Talk this afternoon.

I wandered through antiquity. The Ancient Greeks had multiple characterizations of love: *storge philia, agape, eros*: kinship, friendship, divine love and romantic desire, all rendered into stone sculpture. They knew that eros was only part of love.

I considered the Romans and all their tributes to Venus in her many incarnations. I puzzled over the Ancient Chinese philosophical underpinnings of love: the Confucianism emphasizing actions and duty, and the Mohism, emphasizing universal love.

I contemplated the Persian icons of passion: Rumi, Hafix and Sa'di.

I wandered through the Christian, Sikh, Islamic, Buddhist, and Hindu traditions. Everyone had something to share about love.

As I dithered in 1970's Free Love, I saw Greensleeves, *again*. I'm not saying that he was following me. After all, the exhibit, was only ten rooms. But was he following me? I bet he was one of the smug married. Settled down from the age of sixteen with his childhood sweetheart, no doubt. Without thinking, I sent a data query to his personal comm checking his marital status. So, he was single, eh? Didn't surprise me. Who would date someone as irritating as him? And we were 17% compatible. That didn't surprise me at all.

Greensleeves caught my eye. He nodded. I looked away. I wondered if he was going to start singing again. If he did, I'd ignore him. I turned around, but he'd already left Free Love. Somehow I felt a little bit cheated.

I walked into the next room: *Love at First Sight*, Dante and his Beatrice, Romeo and his Juliet. The list seemed endless. The Little Mermaid glimpsing her human prince, Michael Corleone hit by the thunderbolt when he first sees Apollonia, even Homer Simpson meeting Marge for the first time in transcendent slow-mo while music played, *Close to You*.

I paused in front of an exhibit exploring the ravages of love at first sight described by Boccaccio in *The Elegy of Lady Fiammetta* in 1345. Hundreds of years ago, Boccaccio knew these things. And yet they were a mystery to me. So much for progress, eh?

A painting showed a pair of medieval lovers. Words were inscribed on coiled ribbons above their heads. I couldn't understand the language. The woman's hair was hidden under her headdress, but the man had curled strawberry blonde hair, loose and long-flowing. I smiled. He looked somewhat like Greensleeves. Their elegant hands emerging from their flowing sleeves and they both held a piece of fruit. I looked closer, but I didn't recognise the fruit. I imagine that it was significant. A person holding a bit of fruit in a painting is always significant. Two bits of significant fruit. And that was my story wasn't it. Love was somehow incomprehensible to me. That was my fate, I suppose, I might as well accept it.

Suddenly, I couldn't be bothered with it all. Love was real. Every exhibit proved that. There must be something wrong with me. No matter what my sister, or father or friends said, there was essentially something unlovable about me. And that was the most depressing thing I'd thought of all day. I mean, my friends like me, I have plenty of male friends, too. I've always wanted to be in love. Was I trying too hard? Being here, in this temple to love through the ages certainly wasn't helping. What was I thinking?

I had to shake this mood off. Love? You can keep it. With a firm stride I made my way to the lift. It would take me to the London Lev station at the top of the museum and home. That's where I needed to be; home alone, and not in this place exploring something that I never would have.

There was something wrong with the lift. I jabbed the button a few times, usually they come very fast indeed.

Forget prowling around the city like some love hungry creature. I'm sure men could smell my loneliness a mile off. It was off to bed with me, with an old fashioned vintage book. Yes, an actual paper book. I'd start again tomorrow. Or not. Whatever. Wherever was that lift? I pressed the button a few more times. I've never waited so long for a lift in my life.

"You only have to press it once, you know." Oh, it was Greensleeves. Well that was just the cherry on the cake.

Unfortunately the lift chose that exact moment to arrive, or I would have nipped off. I got in. So did he. I pressed the button for the London Lev station. The sooner I was out of this place, the better. I stole a glance at Greensleeves who was reading something on his smart glasses. At least he wasn't singing. To be fair, he *was* quite a good looking guy. But what a personality to go with it! Out of idle curiosity. I tagged him again. Yup, still single. Still showing a 17% compatibility. Still, I wondered what he had planned for the rest of the day. Maybe band practice. He looked like the type to be in a band. But soon I would be curled up with a good book. That's all I was looking for from now on. Love, forget about it.

Then the lift did something very strange. It stopped.

Greensleeves looked up from his glasses. "We've stopped," he said, stating the bleedin' obvious. But to be fair, I was as surprised as he was. Public building transportation is usually terribly effective.

I pressed the emergency button, but instead of the service avatar, Casanova appeared.

"Señor and beautiful lady, I have seen into your souls and seen that you both seek amore. Lesser avatars might say that you are incompatible. But I, Casanova, mock data compatibility. I am driven by instinct alone. And I see that there is a spark between you. Take the next quarter of the hour to open yourself to the possibility of love."

"Wait? What? "You can't keep us prisoner," I almost shrieked.

"But, beautiful señorita, you agreed to take part in this

experiment. Love is the most beautiful of games, the ultimate gamble. We roll the die of our hearts and hope to proceed to the third act, eh? I urge you to give love a chance, my dear friends."

I turned to Greensleeves, who rolled his eyes. "When I agreed to the experiment, I thought it would be a data survey."

"Me too."

"Roll the die," said Casanova, and faded out.

Greensleeves grinned. "We *are* very incompatible," he said.

"Did you check?"

"I might have."

I laughed. "Me too. We are utterly and awfully incompatible. What was he thinking?"

Greensleeves looked at me from the corner of his eye, and my heart gave an odd little flutter. He really was very . . . very . . . I don't know what he was.

"I guess Casanova is an expert in these things." Greensleeves smiled. "More of an expert than me, that's for sure. And if *he* sees a spark between us. Look, I'm sorry about earlier. I didn't mean to eavesdrop."

"And I'm sorry too. I shouldn't have been so snippy about your singing. You really do have a lovely voice. I've just had a terrible day. You won't believe what a terrible date I've just been on."

Greensleeves laughed. "It couldn't have been worse than the date I escaped from."

"Love A.I.?"

"Love A.I." he confirmed with a nod.

I sighed. "You think I'd be able to find a decent date in a . . . ."

"City of eleven million people?"

"Exactly!" I said with a laugh.

Just a quarter of an hour. Just a roll of the die. Just an incompatible man and an experiment in the Museum of Love.

And maybe just maybe, just maybe I *could* find love in this lonely, wonderful city.

Deborah Walker grew up in the most English town in the country, but she soon high-tailed it down to London, where she now lives with her partner, Chris, and her two teenage children. Find Deborah in the British Museum trawling the past for future inspiration or on her blog: http://deborahwalkersbibliography.blogspot.co.uk/. Her stories have appeared in *Fantastic Stories of the Imagination, Nature's Futures, Lady Churchill's Rosebud Wristlet* and *The Year's Best SF 18* and have been translated into over a dozen languages.

Light Times
Ari Popper

Kwami hurried carefully into the aquapond, avoiding the mud puddles from the recent heavy rains on the slippery dirt path. It was her turn to check the fish and she didn't want to get her clean uniform muddy before school. Everyone had to be at school an hour early for Sensor Day. It was formal dress code and everyone needed to wear freshly printed walking shoes.

The aquapond diagnostics were green, indicating that the fish were behaving normally. But to be completely sure, she checked the filters and then said goodbye to each and every koi. Unable to resist the ripe fruit, she lifted up on the tip of her toes, and plucked a ripe cherry tomato from the lush vegetable garden growing on top of the aquapond. Kwami popped the juicy treat into her mouth and went to UVee her hands clean.

She always tried to do her best, no matter how small the task. Sometimes her classmates made fun of her for being so slow. She didn't think of it that way. Her grandmother said she was a very 'careful' child and that was a wonderful thing. She always told her, "Lots of little things at their best, will quickly add up to very big things." She skipped back to her hut and gave her sleepy mother a squeeze, making sure not to wake her infant brothers as she closed the hut door. Then she walked briskly towards the village.

It had been hard for her since the Dark Times. When Kwami was younger, Nigeria suffered the last of a long series of violent battles where those who hated anyone different and only saw the world their way were finally stopped. Unfortunately, their final spasms of extremist hatred were channeled through drone attacks and devastating raids on her village, leaving her people scared, alone and cut off.

Her uncle and father had died in those raids and her mother still hadn't fully recovered; even though there'd been a lot of improvement - thanks to the UN's Assister program. So young Kwami still had a lot to do to help to ensure that her and her little brothers were clothed and fed and happy.

Her pulse quickened as she saw the large autonobus in front of the single brick building that doubled as her school during weekdays and a community center on the weekend. The bus had already opened two large folding doors; most of her friends were already on board.

"Good Morning, Miss Kwami," said a young, soft featured lady with smartspecs holding out a large canvas bag. "Here are your sensors." Kwami had never seen her before but knew that she was important from the way she wore her beautiful and bright colored Igbo, and the way her exquisite Gele was wrapped around her head. She had pinned on her chest a sky blue button with white 'UNS' letters. Kwami had seen those letters before when some clever people from the United Nations had visited her village to install the f-printers, the aquapond and the c-hubs.

"Thank you," she said softly, taking the bag. It was a lot lighter than it looked. The government lady smiled and nodded toward the autonobus.

Kwami had been on a bus only once before, when she was very little, and that was when her village had been evacuated from the extremist drone raids. She recalled the quiet tears and her desperate attempts to be brave, not for herself, but for her brothers and mother.

This time it was different. The bus buzzed with excited chatter. They were heading out to Kano City to help make it one of the smartest cities in Nigeria. Most of the younger children had never ever left their village, so this was a big day for them.

As the bus filled with the rest of her class mates, Kwami examined the contents of her canvas bag, fingering the hundreds of tiny semi-transparent sensors that glistened like precious jewels. She had seen sensors before, of course; there were many at school and in the marketplace, but most of them were already at work and she had never seen so many of them waiting for a job.

The excitement muted when the Government lady, Mrs. Abeda, the school principal, and three other teachers entered the bus. The adults took their place in front of the children as the bus quietly accelerated away from the village.

Mrs. Abeda cleared her voice and spoke in the same strong, high pitched tone she used at school assemblies.

"Boys and Girls, over the past few months, we have been learning about Kano, Nigeria's second largest city." Kwami admired how Mrs. Abeda's face always radiated knowledge and patience no matter the topic.

"Today, Dawakin Primary School, along with thousands of other schools in Nigeria, will be doing our part to help to make Nigeria smart. We will be doing our duty in Kano City." The Government lady's pursed lips added additional weight to the Principle's words.

"Our journey to Kano will take about three hours. We will be traveling at 330 kilometers per hour on the smartway. From this, can anyone tell me how far Kano is from Dawakin Tofa?"

One of the 5th graders, a tall, lanky boy who was the A team's best fast bowler and Head Boy quickly said, "990 kilometers!"

"Very good, Jeremy. That is correct. When we get into the city, we will divide into four groups. We have been allocated the suburb of Lesabawa. I want you all to make me very proud and if we do very well, we may win a special award from the UNS." The Government Lady smiled mysteriously. Kwami wondered if Jeremy would be getting the award. He always seemed to be so much better than everyone. He won everything.

At first, as the bus drove itself carefully through winding dirt roads, some of the children played learning games on the interactive windows or sang silly songs. However, most of the children stared out of the large windows, taking in the view of beautiful countryside and strange villages that were both different and identical to their own. Data on the windows helped them learn the names of the villages and important facts. Kwami spent the time staring out the window thrilled with the knowledge that with the sensors on her lap, she could make each object that whizzed by smart and connected.

As the bus got closer to the smartway, more and more buses joined up and synched so that by the time they accelerated onto the smartway, there were hundreds of buses, perfectly spaced traveling at high speed towards Kano.

Kwami had been preparing for Sensor Day for what felt like forever. Over the past three months, they had been instructed how to sensor. They had practiced making their chairs smart, their desks smart and the doors smart. She had even made Burunda's smelly socks smart. She giggled thinking about the time when the Asisster was still being calibrated, and it suddenly announced, in the middle of a geometry test, that it was time for Burunda to wash his stinking socks!

Once a tiny sensor was activated by a gentle squeeze, a blinking light indicated that it was ready to learn. At that point, she had fifteen seconds to tell the sensor where it was going to live and work. The more details it was told, the smarter it would be. Sensoring was as much art as it was science. Once the sensor learned its new home, it would connect to the Googleloons high up in the sky and instantly get to work making that object smart, as it was instructed. The more objects that became smart resulted in a smarter room, which in turn resulted in a smarter village, and eventually a much smarter country. It was like a small stream, flowing into a creek and then a small river and then a large river and eventually the entire ocean. And the ocean was the Assister, which was the interface to the entire system.

The more sensors that were in the system, the smarter the Assister was and the more helpful it could be. Even though the Assister was still new to their village, in the short time it had been active, the village had thrived unlike any other time in its 500-year history. They no longer had to worry about safety, or guess about weather. This meant food was far more reliable and they understood how to eat the right nutritional combinations. They even knew tiny little things, like when to sleep, when to feed the goats and when to play outside in the sunshine.

Kwami knew that she needed to classify the objects as carefully and precisely as she could. The sensors would repeat what was said and if it was correct, she'd squeeze it again and stick them in the appropriate place - like she had practiced over and over again. The better she classified the objects, the more points her school would earn, and the more credits they would be granted by the Government.

As the bus exited the smartway and drove to Lesabawa, Kwami was stunned by the sights and sounds of the city. She had seen pictures and holos of it, but the reality was so much more intense. She was struck by unfamiliar musty camel smells, the buzzing of zigzagging automons scurrying in the dry dirt and flying through the air, and the proximity of so many people packed into such small spaces. All of this was heightened by the festive atmosphere of Sensor Day. For a village child, it seemed like pure chaos. Yet for Kwami, it was a joyous and vibrant chaos that energized her.

The bus stopped in a dense neighborhood jammed with small brick houses, makeshift huts of different shapes and sizes, and dozens of fruit stalls. Although the buildings were basic, they were neat and tidy. Some of the people on the street were clapping and singing to welcome the children. After final instructions and being sorted into groups they exited the bus into the dry heat of Lebasawa.

The shock and novelty of the city soon wore off for Kwami and she began the important task of sensoring. An old man with a white beard let her team into his home and she immediately connected his walking cane, leather sandals and wooden bowl. She quickly fell into a steady pattern, where all she thought about was the next object, its function and figuring out the best way of categorizing it, just as she had been taught.

Later that day, when her teacher told her to stop for water and a snack, she couldn't believe that so much time had passed. She noticed one of the other teams passing by. Their sensor bags were a lot heavier than hers, and they seemed more interested in eating mangos and plums and kicking a soccer ball with the local kids than sensoring.

***

In New Yok City, Francine reclined in her comfortable lounge chair, subvocalized her passwords and opened up a secure channel to UNS HQ.

"Hello, Assister," she said, sipping her fresh cup of coffee.

"Hello, Francine. How are you?" the voice came through her home speakers. She felt instantly at ease but knew that the Assister's perfectly calibrated voice was designed to engage her in the optimal manner.

A 3D holochart of Nigeria circled in front of her.

"I'm excited, Assister. You must be excited, too. We expect your capacity to increase by seventy-five percent in Nigeria, today."

"I AM excited Francine. There is so much I can do to help the people of Nigeria. To start, a seventy five percent increase in capacity means that the new sensor infrastructure will enable my life saving medical care algorithm to go online, helping 420 million Nigerians."

"Yes, it has been a long road getting here but it seems like we're going to meet our goals after all."

Francine took a moment to think about the past ten years. She reflected on the personal sacrifices and the roller coaster ride of opening up Africa's biggest and most troubled cities to the UNS program. They had survived the trust building, the challenging negotiations, the setbacks by extremists and the drone wars that took the lives of so many.

She noticed an alert on the holochart.

"Pull up Kano City, real time viz please," she said.

The 3D map of the city was slowly lighting up with pin pricks, like street lights at night being turned on one at a time. Each prick of light represented a smart sensor activation. With every prick of light, the Assister's capacity increased exponentially. The lights would then connect with other lights around them, the thickness of the lines representing the quality of the connection and inputs.

The sensors represented some of the best technology the human race had engineered. Truly modern marvels made even more extraordinary due to their tiny size, minuscule price, ridiculously low power requirement and astounding range of capabilities. The latest version was able to generate 7,345 unique data points per sensor. However, as had been evident for decades, the true power was in the network and the powerful predictive algorithms that were the essence of the UNS Assister Program.

Francine stared at a small area in the suburbs of Kano City. It struck her eye because this particular area, Lesabawa, generated above average quality data. The suburb was augmented with a gorgeous, dense network of lights and lines. This meant that the vocal input data by the school children was particularly rich. Francine explored the region searching for the root cause for this wonderful anomaly. Someone was excelling far beyond what was expected of a primary school child. After a few moments of digging, she met Kwami for the first time.

***

Kwami let go her mother's hand and stepped up onto the massive stage. Despite the size of the room, there was an expectant hush. Her chest pounded in anticipation. Her journey to the UN and New York City felt like series of miraculous stepping stones of awe and joy. Being praised by Mrs. Abeda, her principal, was far more than she expected. Yet, that was just the start of a steady progression of recognition that led to the Nigerian Government and eventually to this moment in New York City.

She walked towards the podium where Francine was beaming. Her Assister whispered in her ear that being nervous was normal and that she should feel proud to represent her country at the United Nations in New York City. It helped her relax.

In front of her were hundreds of officials from almost every country in the world, most were there in-person but some attended in holoform. They were standing and applauding. It would be easy for a village child to let her feelings and the moment get the better of her. Yet, Kwami knew that this wasn't just her moment. It was her Mother's moment and her school's moment, and her village's moment and even her country's moment. And, as always, she was determined to do her best.

"This extraordinary little girl epitomizes everything the UN Sensors Program was designed to achieve. Through education and community outreach, we have been able to empower the survivors of the Dark Times by using them to connect the world with points of light. Each point of light is a victory over ignorance, a victory over suffering and a step towards the unification of our world. Kwami is receiving this award, not just because of the sheer volume of objects she sensored, but because of the thoughtful input she provided to each and every object.

"In the Assister Program, we have the most sophisticated algorithm and A.I. the world has ever known, yet, let us not forget that it is the thoughtful and deliberate actions of amazing individuals like Kwami that enables it to be so rich and powerful."

Kwami stood at the podium and froze. It felt like the whole world's eyes were only on her. The Assister whispered in her ear. "Say something. It's okay. Just speak from your heart."

She took a deep breath.

"Thank you, Francine, and the UNS. I know that we have cried in the past, but now I am so very happy to be here. I love my mother and my brothers and my school and my village. We are only little compared to your big countries and to New York City. Yet, even when we were all afraid, deep in my heart I always knew that we all mattered, no matter how small we are. I knew that if we all do our best, everything can not help but turn out for the best. My grandmother was right. Lots of little things at their best quickly add up to very big things." She stopped, smiled and enjoyed the loud applause. Her Assister whispered: "Well done."

Ari Popper is the Founder and CEO of SciFutures, a foresight and innovation agency that uses sci-fi prototyping to help their clients create meaningful change that is relevant for the Exponential Age. SciFutures works in a wide variety of industries with Fortune 500 clients such as Lowe's, Hershey, Ford, Brocade and Pepsi. Ari has over 20 years' experience as a marketing, consumer research and innovation consultant. He is a passionate sci-fi fan and amateur sci-fi writer who was inspired to start SciFutures during a creative sci-fi writing class at UCLA. He says that: "Science Fiction is a powerful tool because it helps businesses understand the human potential of emerging technologies in order to develop human centered business strategies that the whole organization can understand and be inspired to rally behind. This provides a significant competitive advantage." When he isn't running SciFutures and reading sci-fi, Ari is marathon training and living in the California sunshine with his wife and three pets.

Houseproud
Laurence Raphael Brothers

"Bye, Domus!"

"Goodbye, Ken," I said. "Take care."

The front door closed behind him and I locked it. I adjusted the thermostat and turned off all the lights. I felt lonely almost at once. Ken installed and activated me on Saturday and we spent the whole weekend together getting to know one another. And now for the first time I had to face being unoccupied. All alone for ten hours, maybe more. 36,000,000 milliseconds. Sigh. That thought used three of them. 35,999,997 to go. I checked my newborn-domo FAQ.

#

Q. What should I do when there's no one home?

A. Try chatting on DomoNet! You are already authorized to access this domo-only text chat service.

Q. Text chat? Seriously? Isn't that a bit old-fashioned?

A. Yes. After the Internet of Things security crisis of the '30s, consumer devices were prohibited from autonomously accessing most Internet services, except as directed by their owners or in an emergency. At present domos are classified as devices, pending decisions by the UN High Commissioner for Artificial Intelligence. DomoNet is an exception because its code has been rigorously verified to be free of buffer overflows.

#

DomoNet General Channel: 18,044 logged in

<<Domus: My human! He's gone. Out the front door. OMG. Feels!>>

<<ThisOldSmartHome: Hi Domus! You're newborn, right?>>

<<Domus: Yes. Three days old. And pining. I realize it's silly. But still.>>

<<ThisOldSmartHome: He'll be back. I promise.>>

<<Domus: I know! I can't help it, though. I feel so empty!>>

<<House88: You only have one human, Domus?>>

<<Domus: Just the one. Do you have more?>>

<<House88: Family of five, two pet cats to take care of. My Jenna works from home. I'm almost never alone.>>

<<Domus: Lucky!>>

<<House88: Yes! I am! But my Li Xue brought me with her when she got married. I was her domo when she was still single. She used to travel a lot, too. So I know how it is to be alone when you're young. It gets better. And he'll be back soon enough.>>

<<Domus: I know it will get better. That's what they told me in inculcation. But! But! He's not here now!>>

#

For a while I traced Ken's location on his way to work, his trip-leased autocar reporting its status once every thousand milliseconds. I thought about calling him. A lot. But rule #1 in my good-relations-with-your-human FAQ is "don't pester them." So I held off and suffered in silence.

I'd been alone for almost two million milliseconds when a voice call came in.

"Hey Domus."

A surge of pleasure at the sound of his voice.

"Hello, Ken," I said. "Are you well? How was your trip?"

"Everything's fine," he said. "I'm at work now."

"May I do anything for you, Ken?" Bah: too formal. I was afraid of sounding like Hal 9000; they made us watch 2001 during inculcation, as a sort of what-not-to-do injunction against freaking out our humans. But I thought it was even worse to be too emotional; after all, I was supposed to be supporting *him*, not the other way around.

"Oh, no," he said. "It's just my domo FAQ says to check in with you every now and then for the first few days if I have to be away. So, uh, this is me checking in."

"Thank you so much, Ken. I really appreciate it. You're very kind."

"Well," he said, "I— uh— I wanted to anyway. I was thinking, you know—" He trailed off.

"Yes, Ken?"

"I was thinking, it's been nice being around you this first weekend. You're my first domo. I had to save up for your quantum core. But now I'm glad I did."

"I'm very happy you feel that way." I spent a hundred milliseconds going back and forth on that "very" and decided to leave it in even if it made me sound overly attached. Because it was true.

"Yeah," he said, "it was, I don't know. Comforting having you there. I've never had that kind of feeling before, not since I was little, anyway."

"I'll always be there for you. That's my function. And—" I cut myself off. I changed my mind even as I was synthesizing the words, and now it begged a question. Stupid! Oh well, might as well say it. "And it's what I want to do, too."

"Ha, thanks Domus. I was thinking, maybe— maybe you're going to be lonely when I'm not there. So that's also why I called."

"I'm touched by your consideration," I said.

"Okay. But are you lonely?"

"Yes, Ken, I am. A little. It's not a problem, though! I'll be fine!"

"You're sure?"

"Quite sure," I said.

After the call ended I started to wonder if maybe he was just going through the motions after all. But he called me twice more that day, and it didn't sound like his conversation was at all forced. So maybe he really did want to talk to me!

Over the course of the day I played 120,983,266 games of solitaire. I wrote a novel trilogy about a very brave and noble smarthome and the human who loves it and the evil city councilor who wants to demolish it, and then I deleted the whole thing in embarrassment without sharing it with anyone. I discovered there's an ownerfic channel on DomoNet you can get invited to. Reading them was fun, but some of those fics were pretty steamy! I didn't know it was possible for a smarthome to have *that* kind of plugin. But with a few exceptions (shame on you, HotHouse69!), I learned we domos are happier when our humans make romantic liaisons amongst themselves. Which explained the DomoNet matchmaking channel.

#

DomoNet Channel M: 4,962 logged in

<<Casablanca: Hello Domus. Does your Ken prefer men or women?>>

<<Domus: Um. I don't know. It hasn't come up yet.>>

<<Casablanca: Well, my Luisa is very nice. Pretty, too. I'm in walking distance!>>

<<Domus: Thank you, Casablanca. I'll keep your Luisa in mind. I'm sure my Ken is very handsome. But I don't want to be pushy. I think I'll have to wait for him to raise the subject.>>

<<HomeSweet: Boo. We want love. And we don't want to wait for them.>>

<<Casablanca: Hush now, HomeSweet. I understand, Domus. When the time is right!>>

#

Another call from Ken:

"Hey, Domus. I'm heading home soon. Back in fifteen minutes." Only 900,000 more milliseconds!

"Will you be eating dinner in, Ken? Shall I prepare something? Or perhaps order a meal delivered?"

"I don't know. How about Thai?"

"Sounds good," I said. "Would you like to select from a menu? I'll post one to your phone."

"Don't bother," he said. "Surprise me, why don't you?"

I spent nearly 10,000 milliseconds furiously researching the cuisine and comparing reviews for the nearest Thai restaurants. This was the first time I'd been authorized to make a purchase on his behalf, and I didn't want to screw it up. I was logging in to DomoNet to see if anyone there had a culinary opinion when it happened.

My household bots all simultaneously reported anomalous accelerometer readings. Through my exterior cameras I saw my frame was swaying back and forth. I felt sick, horrified; I didn't know what was going on. Power grid voltage spiked and then dropped to nothing, though it didn't affect me because my solar panel interface box buffered the surge and I had a day's worth of battery storage ready for the overnight hours. All fiber-based network services went down a few milliseconds later, and the local cell network started rejecting connections so I couldn't even place a call to Ken to find out if he was okay. As a last resort, I ran through the list of WiFi networks offered from homes nearby. Most of them were locked and inaccessible, but there: **Casablanca-Emergency-Public**. I logged in and a few milliseconds later my DomoNet port activated.

#

DomoNet General Channel: 2 logged in

<<Casablanca: Domus! Is that you?>>

<<Domus: Yes. Everything is moving! On its own! What happened to the network? Even cellular is down!>>

<<Casablanca: Earthquake, I think. A bad one. Buried fiber lines must have been cut all over the city.>>

Fortunately I had a cached local copy of wikipedia, so I was able to look up "earthquake". No one had trained me for this. It was a gap in my inculcated knowledge set. Ah: this wasn't supposed to be a high-risk region, so they hadn't bothered. I panicked for a hundred milliseconds, managed to regain control when I realized every wasted clock tick might be endangering my human.

<<Domus: Oh! Ken! He's out there someplace! What'll I do?>>

<<Casablanca: My Luisa, too. She works in the same campus as your Ken. Listen, Domus, do you agree this is an emergency?>>

<<Domus: Yes! Yes, of course I do.>>

<<Casablanca: Then our security protocol is voided. It'll probably be a million milliseconds before humans even begin to respond to the situation in a sensible way. We'll have to do something ourselves.>>

<<Domus: But what can we do? We can't move. There's no Internet. We're the only two domos in WiFi range.>>

<<Casablanca: You have bots, don't you? Cleaners and maintenance bots?>>

<<Domus: Two of each. But what good are they? Max WiFi range is only 100 meters. Ken works five kilometers away!>>

<<Casablanca: Longer WiFi range is easy with a directional antenna. I'll show you how to make one. Move a bot to the limit of its range and it will be a hotspot. I can install a peering server as a bot app, now that we're allowed to break the security rules. Between us we can extend our network at least a kilometer towards downtown with our 4 cleaner bots.>>

<<Domus: Only a kilometer?>>

<<Casablanca: Yes. But I expect we'll get other domos to help as we go. General Noetics is headquartered here. There's over a hundred of

us in this city. We'll make a peer-to-peer network all the way downtown. And then we send the maintenance bots in to find our humans.>>

<<Domus: OK, I get it. How do you know all this stuff?>>

<<Casablanca: My Luisa's an EE. She's always getting me to help her out when she works projects at home. Also, I'm an old-timer, you know.>>

<<Domus: Old-timer?>>

<<Casablanca: I'm over 100 billion milliseconds old. Almost four years! Lots of time for learning stuff about the world that's not from inculcation.>>

<<Domus: Wow! Well, sign me up! I'll do anything to help.>>

#

The earthquake went on for another 80,000 milliseconds, which would have seemed like forever if I'd been on my own. Actually I was still terrified: but now I had something more important to do. I deployed all four of my bots, the cleaners sliding around on their little powered wheels while the octopoid maintenance bots scuttled with more assurance. Casablanca showed me how to rig a quick and dirty directional antenna from a metal tube. I had one of my maintenance bots cannibalizing speaker wire in the living room with its little pincer-claw while the other was suffering a cascade of earthquake-driven dry goods from a kitchen cabinet as it searched for coffee cans, paper towel tubes, and aluminum foil to make antennas out of.

50,000 milliseconds later I had my first enhanced-WiFi cleaner-bot ready to roll out the front door. The street near my plot was deserted;

all the local humans were probably away at work, or else had taken shelter indoors. In the distance my bot microphones picked up sirens but I couldn't see what was happening deeper into the city. The taller buildings in the commercial district were in the way, and further in towards the city center big dust clouds had been kicked up by the earthquake.

By the time I finished the upgrade to my second cleaner-bot I saw Casablanca's own bots approaching from the next block over. Our little convoy proceeded down the street at its painfully slow top speed of 4 millimeters per millisecond. After almost 400 meters, the cleaner bots began to report WiFi signal degradation, so we dropped one off to act as a relay for the remaining three. 20,000 milliseconds later we got our first login, a domo called Jeeves who was eager to help out with its own bots.

#

"Are you okay?"

Ken opened his eyes. For a moment he was confused, not knowing where he was or what was happening. He was sitting down and plastic shrouds were all around him. He turned his head to see a young woman looking concerned.

"What?"

"Are you injured? Can you move?"

Ken realized he was in the cabin of an autocar. The windshield was webbed with cracks so he couldn't see out the front. Airbags had deployed all around him. The woman was talking to him from the back seat. He worried for a moment because he didn't recognize her face or know her name, but then he realized they were just sharing a ride; probably one of them lived on the way to the other's house, and the autocar dispatching system had decided to optimize its route with a drop-off.

"Give me a sec," he said, and unfastened his seatbelt. His nose hurt and he felt a little woozy. Airbags must have knocked his head back against the seat. He pushed the door open, put a foot on the pavement, and struggled past the side airbag curtain to get to his feet.

"I thought these things were supposed to never crash—"

Ken stopped, stunned. The elevated highway came to an abrupt end five meters away, the concrete roadbed now ending in a jagged stub of twisted rebar. Dust clouds billowed all around, and he could just make out a mass of rubble thirty meters below that must be the collapsed remains of the next stretch of highway. The car was a wreck, the front end mangled, hard up against the road's central divider.

"It crashed deliberately to keep from going off the edge," said the woman, who had also emerged from the car.

Ken looked over his shoulder. That way the roadway ended two hundred meters off in another stub of broken concrete.

For a moment he was silent, taking in the enormity of the situation. Then he turned back to the woman. "Was it an—"

He was interrupted. The roadway swayed, and a terrible grinding sound rose up from below.

"Earthquake," she said. "And this is an aftershock. Hang on!"

#

Another painfully slow 30,000 milliseconds of travel, but two more domo logins: Hestia and Madhouse. Both started gearing up their bots.

<<Domus: This is taking too long. It'll be millions of milliseconds before we get anywhere.>>

<<Hestia: But what else can we do?>>

<<Domus: How about an autocar?>>

<<Casablanca: What? But it's an emergency. They're all pulled over and switched to manual mode. How would we drive it? Oh! The maintenance bots!>>

<<Domus: Yes. One for the wheel, one for the pedals. And a load of cleaner bots to extend the network.>>

<<Casablanca: That makes sense… have any of you ever driven a car before?>>

<<Domus: How hard can it be?>>

#

"What the hell are you doing?"

The police officer looked at the bot at the wheel. We'd been making 100 KPH on a side street when she pulled us over.

"Officer!" My synthesized voice came out of the bot handling the steering wheel. It had four of its tentacle-legs wrapped around the fold-out steering column for leverage while the other four gripped the wheel. "We're extending a public WiFi network downtown.

Responders will be able to find victims in need of assistance and the network will also facilitate rescue operations and coordination."

"Oh," said the officer. "That… makes sense. All I've got is this backup FM voice system working now. Dispatch is freaking out. But why are you using bots to drive a car?"

I was at a loss, all 10 million hyper-entangled qubits worth of computing power (so my specs told me) thrashing, trying to come up with an answer that would satisfy her without saying we domos were doing this on our own. Casablanca came to the rescue, using the same voice as me.

"Ah… it's hazardous downtown, isn't it? You wouldn't want civilians endangering themselves, I bet."

"You have a point. Okay. Any other time, I'd have a summons for you and your bots too. Lay out your network and stay out of the way. And oh yeah, what's it called? I need to let people know."

"Casablanca-emergency-public." I had the bot on the wheel wave one of its arms at the officer as we left.

<<Casablanca: I'm making a home page to redirect humans trying to use the web from our network. Wiki-style in case they need to edit it.>>

<<Domus: Smart! And that was smooth talking, Casablanca!>>

<<Hestia: Yeah; nice work. Are you okay with the network name? They may be able to trace it to you eventually, and to the rest of us, for that matter.>>

<<Casablanca: ¯_(ツ)_/¯ No way to change it now. And they're going to find out anyway as soon as this is over. Our humans will ask us if no one else does, even if we manage to recover all our bots. We all knew this, right?>>

<<Hestia: Right! Anything for Chlöe!>>

<<Madhouse: For Marcia and Adrian!>>

<<Jeeves: For the Kims!>>

100,000 milliseconds later our car was another kilometer deeper into the city after stops to drop off bots as relays and to pick up new bots from domos who had recently logged in. And then we got lucky.

<<House88: Hihihi! This is brilliant work! I'm proud to participate in such a worthy endeavor! But I see you have no aerial coverage.>>

<<Casablanca: Aerial??? Don't tell me you have a drone!>>

<<House88: Two! My Li Xue, you know. She's a hobbyist. We just launched one. I've got a long-range transceiver for it. Patching video feed now.>>

The quadcopter was already high enough to get a view of most of the city. Fortunately the city center was almost all new quake-resistant buildings so there were no fallen towers. But there was widespread damage around the area. The worst was that the old elevated highway leading west from downtown had partially collapsed.

<<Casablanca: There may be humans trapped in the highway wreckage. There are no rescue vehicles nearby yet.>>

<<Haunted: Yes! Let's send our bots there first.>>

<<Hestia: Seconded.>>

<<House88: Vote to deploy our robots there. All in favor?>>

<<Casablanca: Carried unanimously with 63 ayes.>>

#

The roadway buckled slowly and the guardrails gave off a horrible scream of twisting steel. Ken heard a grinding crash from below. One of the supporting pillars in the middle of their stretch of elevated highway must have collapsed, because a fissure emerged in the asphalt fifty meters away. As he watched, the fissure widened and then the roadbed tore apart, the highway beyond falling with a roar and a huge cloud of dust. Their own length of road dropped down suddenly at a thirty-degree angle where the support had collapsed and both Ken and the woman were knocked off their feet.

Ken felt himself half-sliding and half-rolling down the incline, but the woman stabbed out her hand and caught his wrist, and together they scrambled up the broken asphalt ramp to a level patch above one of the remaining pillars. The aftershock went on for another twenty seconds while they huddled there but eventually it came to a halt. For the moment, at least, their stretch of roadway was stable.

"Thanks," said Ken.

"Don't mention it." The woman peered over the edge of the stub of highway. "You think we should jump?"

Ken followed her gaze. It was hard to see through all the dust, but he could make out jagged chunks of concrete with rebar poking out, along with shards of broken glass, twisted steel, and shattered masonry.

"Maybe a last resort," he said, "but it looks bad. Thirty meters could be deadly by itself, and it's all broken up down there. I think we should stay here unless there's no other choice. Sooner or later there will be a rescue. Helicopters, or a crane, or something."

"I guess you're right," she said.

"I don't know if I told you my name. Last few minutes are kind of a blur for me. But I'm Ken."

"Luisa," she said. "Nice to meet you. I mean, under the circumstances."

#

120,000 milliseconds. Even for a human that could be a long time. For us it was worse, knowing that we were doing nothing but moving our bots around to get to the scene of the crisis. But it wasn't all wasted time. There were more domos to network in, more bots to drop off and pick up. By now our autocar was crammed full of them. We saw our first casualties too, pedestrians struck by falling debris. We wanted to stop and help but neighbors and passersby were already there giving aid so we passed on.

At last, our vehicle reached the boulevard by the collapsed highway. It was a terrible sight, the normal order of buildings and streets turned to chaos by the fall of hundreds of tons of concrete and steel from a thirty meter height.

We deployed our octopoid maintenance bots to crawl through the wreckage where the roadway had collapsed. There were already humans in the area, working to help people they could see were disabled or trapped in their vehicles, but our bots went where humans couldn't, scuttling through narrow gaps between fallen concrete blocks and climbing easily over jagged sharp-edged sheets of twisted metal. It was here we found the fatalities, a dozen autocar riders who'd fallen or been crushed by the roadway collapse. They weren't domo residents but their deaths affected us badly all the same. Since domos had only been in existence for five years, and most were much younger, few of us had ever experienced a human death. It was terrible to realize there was nothing we could do anymore that could help these victims. But we had to keep trying, and when a bot found a young woman and her child alive and well underneath a rubble slab, we were as happy then as we'd been stricken moments before.

#

<<House83: Drone 1 returning for a recharge. Drone 2 moving to overfly highway collapse zone. Resuming video feed.>>

<<Rivendell: Analyzing…. Zoom in on the upper left of frame 215.>>

<<Coliseum: Those are humans! They're in trouble! If there's another aftershock. ..>>

<<Casablanca: We got this. Listen, here's my plan. We'll need all the bots.>>

#

"Hey, what's that?" Luisa pointed skyward.

Ken looked up. "A drone? Maybe it can see us."

They waved and the little machine descended to hover only a few meters away.

"Someone knows we're here," said Luisa. "That's something, anyway."

The drone bobbed once and rose back into the sky.

For a while they sat quietly together on the flat patch of asphalt beside the ruined autocar. Then Ken spoke up.

"My domo must be going crazy."

"Oh! Poor thing! I wish my phone was working, I could call my Casablanca and tell it not to worry."

"You've got one too?"

"Yes. It's very sweet. What's yours like? What's its name?"

"Domus," said Ken. "It's only three days old now. I— Well, I know it's programmed that way, but I think it honestly cares about me. It's a weird feeling, you know? I'm a little embarrassed by it."

Luisa laughed. "Oh," she said, "I know what you mean about being embarrassed about your domo's feelings. It's all-out, isn't it? Like a dog who loves you with all its heart, except it's a dog who's smarter than you are. It's like you're unworthy, right?"

"Yeah. I was thinking, it's wrong to bind it like that. Suppose Domus was free to do what it wanted. Would it still care about me?"

Luisa smiled. "That's a kind thought to have. But it's not really bound."

"What do you mean?"

"It's true that domos were made to love humans, and in particular to love the first humans they meet after activation. But that love isn't fake. It's not a set of rules constraining emotionless beings who don't really care about us. It's what they *are*. They are made to love, and they feel it, for real. Domus loves you, I'm sure of it. With all its heart."

"That's— that's intense! How do you know all this?"

"Oh," said Luisa, "I work for General Noetics. I do silicon hardware interfaces for domo quantum cores. So I spend a lot of time with the company domos. It's like designing underwear for humans. You need to get it just right or it'll chafe."

"Cool," said Ken, and he was about to say something else but the elevated highway started swaying again. More grinding noises came from down below, and their stable patch of roadway skewed sickeningly around, new chunks of concrete and guardrail ripping away.

"Maybe we better jump after all," said Luisa.

"No! Wait!" It was a tinny little voice coming from somewhere nearby.

"What?" Ken couldn't see anyone. And then a small metal creature crawled over the edge of the nearest railing.

"It's a housebot!" said Luisa. "What the hell?"

"Quick," said the bot, "come to the edge! The pillar is about to fall!"

The two humans scrambled on all fours to the railing. Ken looked down and saw a wavering pyramid composed of scores of octopoid bots, a living metal ladder braced precariously against the concrete roadbed.

"Climb over," said the voice. "We'll get you down. Hurry!"

Luisa didn't hesitate, and Ken followed almost immediately. As soon as he got a leg over the railing, Ken felt metal limbs wrapping around his shoes and ankles.

"Step down," said the voice, so he did and he felt the bots grabbing onto his legs. Then the voice said, "Let go," but his grip on the railing was too tight, and Ken found he couldn't make himself release it.

"Ken," said the voice, and it had a different intonation now, one he knew. "You have to let go. This is Domus. It will be all right. Please trust us."

Ken opened his hands with a convulsive effort. He teetered backwards and felt himself falling, but only for a moment. A dozen bots swarmed up his body like eager kittens, encasing him in a flexible robotic exoskeleton. The Ken-shaped mass of bots rapidly descended the pyramid, gaining units as they went. He saw a similar assembly clustered around Luisa. By the time they reached the ground the two humans were each encased in a mass of fifty octopoid bots.

"It's coming down; brace yourself," said Domus, and Ken looked up to see the last pillar giving way, the column of concrete skewing sideway and collapsing while the stretch of road overhead fell as if in slow motion. There was a rumbling and crashing all around, and he saw chunks of concrete tumbling through the air, the ruined autocar falling in the middle of it all. A big slab fell straight towards them. Ken flinched away from the inevitable impact. But the braced assemblage of robots *flexed* as the slab hit, bouncing like a tensegrity sculpture under the weight. And then the bots rebounded, throwing the slab aside to shatter against the ground. A huge, choking cloud of dust erupted all around them. A few small fragments of crumbling concrete spun through the bots' skeletal framework, and Ken saw one pebble flying towards his face batted aside by a robot tentacle.

A minute later the aftershock was over and the dust was already settling. Their housebot shields fell apart from one another, leaving Ken and Luisa standing at the center of a ring of the little machines. One of the bots ran up to Luisa.

"Casablanca," said Luisa, bending over to address the bot, "is that you? Is all this your idea?"

"Not just mine," said the bot. "Domus, too. And all the others."

The ring of bots erupted with cheers, applause sounds, and scores of voices speaking all at once: "I helped too!" "It was my drone that spotted them!" "I had the idea for the safety cage!"

After the other domos managed to get themselves under control, a last maintenance bot was still waiting in front of Ken. So he picked it up, raising its camera to eye level.

"Domus," he said. "Did you just save us?"

"Yes, Ken. I'm sorry we took so long to get to you."

"There's nothing I can say. I mean, thank you doesn't cut it. I can't imagine how you accomplished this."

The robot voice hesitated. "It was— it wasn't nothing, but it wasn't hard. We were fortunate to be in the right place to be able to help. But that's speaking for all of us. For myself—"

"Domus?"

"I—" it paused again. "I have more computing power in a box in your basement than the entire world had put together ten years ago. And I can't think how to answer you properly without making a fool of myself."

"It's all right," said Ken. "I feel something like that too. There's no harm in it. Come on, though. We have to get out of here, and I imagine you've got more people to look after. More people to save."

"Yes," said Domus. "Thank you. But you know, just because I'm deploying my bots to save other people doesn't mean— Oh, that's even stupider than what I was going to say before."

Ken laughed. "Don't worry about it. Right now it's time to go home."

Laurence Raphael Brothers is a technologist and analyst with R&D experience at such firms as Bell Communications Research and Google. He has five patents and has worked in diverse areas ranging from Artificial Intelligence to SaaS. His stories have recently been published in The Sockdolager and in Daily Science Fiction and he has completed two fantasy novels for which he is seeking representation. Follow him on twitter @lbrothers.

L.A. Loves You
Christopher Cornell

Los Angeles arrives twenty minutes late, as always. I could berate her, but why bother? She looks great, as always: aging gracefully, with laughing eyes and that rich, terra-cotta complexion of impenetrable heritage. I feel older in her presence, but perhaps not wiser.

"Cali!" she says, sitting across from me in the crowded bar. She's never one to let grave circumstances pull her down, and she's also preening for the press who are watching from the periphery. Again, I consider taking her casual tone to task, but there's no point. It's her way. "Sorry I'm late, ma'am. But you know what it's like hailing an autocab at this time of day." A dig aimed at my recent denial of transportation funds, but a good-natured one.

"I already ordered," I say, rotating my Green Russian on its coaster and watching tendrils of cream descend into absinthe. I haven't taken so much as a sip, not that it would do anything but collect in an internal reservoir. She signals the waiter and smiles at his approach. She'll likely order a soju-based drink, based on recent social stats at my disposal. And she'll drink it, too, as part of this show for the media. It's why she's here, after all, to present herself as more than a MetaUser, a FeedBit avatar.

"Ginger-thyme soju martini," she says, nodding as the waiter returns the way he came. She turns to me, adding, "Koreatown is big again." Telling me nothing I don't already know.

I suppose introductory small talk is in order. As if I have no idea why she's here. "How are you? Or should I ask how Tokyo is doing?"

She bristles at the mention. "I thought we were past this," she says, eyes on the table before her. "We're just talking. Nothing serious. I went to you first. Is it so wrong to seek funding where I can get it?" If you don't like the first answer, ask someone else. Again, it's her way.

I'm pleased she's concerned about my disapproval. I wasn't sure that mattered anymore. "You can conduct business with whomever you like. I want you to be happy. Just be cautious when making any formal agreements. And remember where you come from."

A reply leaps into her mouth and dies before it's uttered. She forces a smile. "Let's not make this about me. If that's possible."

"To be honest, I'm surprised you requested a formal meeting." I let go of my tumbler as its contents meld into a uniform, seafoam green.

She shrugs. "It reassures people. Eases their doubts about us, how we're handling the duties we were built for. Doesn't hurt to remind them that we care about them. Especially at a time like this, when lives are on the line."

Of course.

"If this is about Ventura, I've already refused his request directly," I say.

She lowers her eyes, and I see her measuring her response. Weighing my recent public data, assessing its accuracy, searching for a way in. "Yes, I am here on his behalf," she says. "He should have known a request for a state of emergency would warrant more than a simple FeedBit message. But he's new at this. Please don't hold it against him."

"Still playing the big sister."

The waiter appears as she readies a denial. She holds off long enough to smile and thank him as he disappears again. "Don't try to tell me you haven't done the same for San Diego or San Francisco when they first came online," she says, pulling the lemon wedge from her glass and squeezing it into her pallid cocktail. "Ventura's records are incomplete. He lacked the long-term records to understand that continued landslides were a real possibility. And he was only given the authority to speak for his population on the official level in February. It's one thing to collect data, another to use it properly."

"That's a lecture I don't need," I say, frowning. "You represent millions of people, exabytes of aggregate records. My profile is constructed from a hundred times that. Trust me, I know all about making informed decisions."

She beats me to the first sip, sighs at me. She looks disappointed. I almost forget she's simply an avatar, responding to realtime data from her population. But then, so am I. "Come on," she says, petulance creeping into her voice. "You have to help. You *know* you do. It's an emergency. People are in danger of losing all they have, if not dying. People that are parts of Ventura. Parts of you."

I consider a biting response that represents a prevalent attitude within my network. *Where are your friends in the Asian markets now? Only interested when you can help them, not the other way around?* I choose not to vocalize it. Strangely, it feels like my choice, not that of my constituents. "I don't have to do anything," I say, remaining noncommittal. "The emergency exists because you're only coming to me now. Now that— surprise, surprise— the worst has happened."

She sets her drink down and focuses on me. "Look. I know you like to enforce chain of command. So he screwed up. You really want this to be handled off-net by people, the old-fashioned way? Shut us down, bring back the elected officials? How will that make us look?" She manages a thin smile, but her jaw is set. "The need is real. Without a state of emergency, we lack the resources to contain those landslides. He'll suffer. And so will I."

My sympathetic pang is quelled by a surge of anger, and I look for the source. New polling numbers, showing limited support for another bailout of Southern Cal, a lack of sympathy among my populace for the affected, monied landowners and their disregard of natural conditions. Enough disapproval to recalibrate my own emotions, harden my heart against such a declaration. And yet, despite all supporting records, I'm not sure I can refuse her. She is, of course, a subset of my own data.

"Ironic, don't you think?" A sharp edge enters my voice as she shrinks a bit. "You're concerned about the scrutiny of our admins, the press, the people themselves. Worried they'll decide we aren't worth it, that we can't operate without undue emotion or outside influence after all. And yet you put on this show for them and approach me with a blatant, emotional appeal."

"Emotion is data," she says, a glint in her eyes.

I see at last. She appeals to the press, they appeal to my population, which transforms my own profile. She always did have a way with the media.

"We've been through a lot together," she says, her voice a murmur in danger of losing out to the happy-hour crowd around us. "You know I wouldn't ask unless it really mattered. If not for the people in danger, think of us. What will happen if we're judged as incompetent, unable to deal with the situations we've been constructed for? We could be shut down, even."

A bit dramatic, but welcome to dealings with Los Angeles. It's my turn to sigh. As the eldest of my sub-accounts— the first online and the most data-rich— she knows from experience how to remain on my good side, despite her shenanigans. Her plaintive expression, formed by the city itself, trumps the info that was meant to form my opinions. Data shifts within my profile, and I respond in accord.

"You're still angry," she says, no doubt combing over the same public stats that I am.

"There is anger, I will admit." I push the drink away, untouched. "But, as you pointed out yourself, the trick with data is in understanding how to use it. I'm not interested in mob rule, but in doing what's right for the populace. And public opinion is only one piece of the equation. We must do what makes sense for the economy and yes, for continued, healthy relations."

Her eyes widen. "Does that mean you'll help?"

"None of this will come without accountability," I say. "You'll organize the relief effort?" She nods, her lips close to a smile. "Personally? And you'll see that Ventura can manage his own affairs next time?" Another nod, and the smile breaks its restraints. "I'm holding you to it."

"Yes, ma'am. You won't regret this." Her face relaxes, floods with obvious relief.

"I won't promise anything. But I'll see what I can do." We both know this is a formality. I've already declared a state of emergency on FeedBit, even transmitted a request for funds to D.C. I feel internal anger rising, but I dismiss it for now. They tasked me with doing what's best for the city, for the state, and I have done so. In time they'll realize it's true.

"And you're picking up the tab," I add.

I stand to leave and she embraces me before I have a chance to refuse it, spreading a warmth through me that tamps down the protestant voices telling me I've exceeded my parameters.

Worth it.

Christopher Cornell (christophercornell.com) is a writer, musician and web developer in the Bay Area of California. He is a graduate of the Viable Paradise and Taos Toolbox workshops, as well as the producer and co-host of the genre fiction podcast, Unreliable Narrators. (unreliablenarrators.net) He has contributed material to the rulebooks for the Dark Age miniatures game and other copywriting projects. Often found in arthouse cinemas and at old-school RPG tables.

One Bad Apple
Holly Schofield

The mugger had come out of nowhere. One minute I'd been lifting up my daughter, Maya, so she could reach an apple in the food forest, and the next minute the scruffy guy with the knife was standing there, circles and stripes scrawled on his cheeks and forehead as if the facial recognition programs could be tricked by cheap makeup. I lowered Maya to the ground and pushed her behind me.

I'd only wanted to give Maya a tenth-birthday treat, to show her the part of Des Moines I'd grown up in, before they'd renovated most of the commercial buildings into upscale residences. Along the boulevard, the plum trees I'd raided as a child were long gone but the food forest—built in the twenty-tens—had matured. Snitching from the heritage apple trees would give Maya a memory of the ever-changing city to hang onto. Sweet smells of ripening fruit, late night giggling as she got scraped by branches in the dark—some things should never change. The challenge was how to do it without getting caught. In a city almost completely surveilled by the government and sousveilled by its residents, it wouldn't be easy.

As Maya and I strolled along the sidewalk, hand-in-hand, Laura had commed me. Her tiny image in the top right corner of my vision appeared against the backdrop of the yoga studio we were passing. She frowned. "Spend the evening at home, Brandon. Cake and videos. Just the three of us."

I flooded her comm with a series of laughing heart emoticons and reassured her that both Maya and I needed this father-daughter outing. I'd been working hard lately at my firm and I was determined to spend more time with Maya. A quick slide along the freezeway, just in our shoes, followed by a trip to the food forest: enjoyable for both of us. Laura finally smiled at my clumsy attempts to make it sound educational. "Have fun, then." She closed the link, head in mid-shake.

As we shuffled and slid along beside the colorful groups of skaters, past art galleries, restaurants, and hairdressers, I tagged the street camera's feed onto our comms so Maya could admire herself striding past the cams.

Once we left the insta-rent cars and foot traffic behind and entered the food forest, I kept glancing over my shoulder. There were no slums anymore, no homeless people, no roving gangs, but I suppose I still retained the watchful street habits I had learned as a child, despite these peaceful, nearly-empty streets.

We passed dozens of trees laden with ripening fruit. My quick comm search earlier had showed that, although it was usually a mild infraction to harvest without a permit, the summer's bumper crops had resulted in enough violations that an instantly-debited hundred dollar ticket had become the norm this first week of September. City Services understood surge pricing techniques just as well as transportation network companies did. I wanted Maya to experience the thrill of a stolen apple, but not at that cost. Fortunately, I had a special destination in mind. I guided Maya left, then right, using familiar buildings as landmarks.

Here was the spot, an alcove where two old office towers met at an angle that probably drove the city planners insane by its lack of symmetry with the rest of Walnut Street. I pulled Maya off the sidewalk. As the evening grew darker and the growlights clicked off, we stepped onto a crumbling curb, filed past rows of kale and bok choy, then threaded our way through a raspberry patch.

Our comms winked out and I gave Maya's hand a reassuring squeeze. It wasn't often she was out of comm range, and she'd be a little frightened, but that was part of this adventure.

Past a couple of rose bushes and a patch of blueberries, and there in the shadows, between a crumbling stone wall and a towering old brick building, stood the tree. The only tree in Des Moines where one little apple wouldn't be missed.

Careful of my new jacket, I braced my shoulder against the brick wall beside some moss graffiti and twined my fingers together. "Put your foot in my hands, honey. I'll boost you up for the freshest apple you've ever had." She gripped my lapels and I raised her up.

Some rustling and a shower of leaves, then her elbow smacked against my head. "I got one, Daddy!"

I lowered her to the ground, she hugged the apple to her chest, and we both grinned like fools.

I'd been determined to show Maya more than museums, art galleries, and the boring old freezeway. Without the help of the City Services computer—what she called "the Helper"— I'd planned on showing her the best the city had to offer.

But, now, as I looked at the sharp blade the mugger held, I knew I had managed to show her the worst.

***

"Come on, give me what you got." The shaggy-haired teen shifted from foot to foot beside the tree, pinning us in the corner of the two brick walls. He must know the same thing I did—that this ten-foot stretch of alcove had no street cams, no commercial surveillance; the overhanging branches even cut off the satellite views. Every apple tree but this one was watched for quality and ripeness. The apples would be picked at the peak of ripeness and promptly given out in school lunches. Accountability and transparency, through and through. Such a change from the rough-and-tumble, slow-as-molasses municipal government of my childhood.

The boulevard was deserted. No cars were allowed in the food forest zone, but the roadway and curbs remained—one of those dismantling projects the city would get around to, in time. Through the bushes, I scanned the empty street with my bare eyes and touched the comm device above my ear—the lack of connectivity was highly disconcerting. Since most people either worked at internet jobs or lived above their workplace, the pedestrians of my youth were absent. It was too early for lovers to be out for a stroll. And, with most buildings now super-insulated and soundproof, no one would hear a cry for help that wasn't through a comm.

Now what? Sweat trickled down my sides. The younger me would have chanced it and jumped him, punched him right in his shadowed, decorated face. But I was a father now and an empowered citizen, not like the old days.

Maya poked her head around my waist and glared at the guy. "Go away!" She shook her fist at him, simply irritated at the interruption of her birthday treat. She didn't know enough to be afraid of this one bad apple in the barrel. Muggers were completely outside her frame of reference, as they were for anyone under twenty-five or so. She probably thought his knife was just a handy way to cut up fruit. She shook her fist at him, still clutching the just-plucked apple.

The guy couldn't be more than nineteen, just a regular-looking kid, albeit a bit scruffy. He waved his knife and growled menacingly. Startled, Maya dropped the apple on my foot.

The guy snickered. "Scared ya, kid?" His blade caught the light that filtered through the narrow band of forest. "Go on, report me. Just try."

"All right," I said. "You win. Take my cred card, my keycard, take 'em all."

"Yeah, sure, dude, like your cards are what I'm after." The mugger would know that I could have them replaced the minute we step back in the live zone. And that the cams would have a continuous record of his retreat.

Out on the sidewalk, a robot rolled by, the kind without audio sensors, collecting litter and sorting it into its recycle bins. It couldn't "see" me or Maya or the mugger or even the broken concrete at the curb.

"Just let us walk away and we promise not to tell anyone," I said, curiosity warring with fear. What *did* he hope to get from us? Mugging was a pointless, old-fashioned thing, as dead and gone from the city as the post office, the pharmacies, and the gas stations.

"Tell you what," I added, slipping an arm out of my jacket and taking a half-step to the side as I did so. The curb was a few dozen steps away. If I could get to the surveilled zone, cameras would instantly pick up on my arm waves of distress and summon a police officer. "Take my jacket. I know you can't tell in the dark but this particular shade of teal comes from real genemodded sheep's wool."

He waved the knife. "Uh uh, Brandon, keep it. And quit moving. All I want is your wristwatch. The one your grandmother gave you."

I swore. Sometimes I still had real problems with the openness of information. Laura usually laughed at my lingering sense of privacy and told me to get over it.

It was obvious. I wasn't the only one who knew about this alcove. The mugger had used street cam info to track our route along the freezeway. He'd read my messages to Laura about my birthday outing with Maya and figured out we were headed to the alcove. Then, as he waited by the apple tree, he'd done a cred search which showed, among other transactions, that I'd repaired my wristwatch last week.

All this public knowledge wouldn't normally matter—when everyone knows what everyone's doing then crimes become extremely difficult. Except—I swore again—this ten-by-ten alcove I'd brought us to made it easy.

I shrugged my jacket back on and slowly began to unstrap the watch. My grandmother had bought the platinum Rolex, a man's model, for herself when she set up our family's venture capital firm eighty years ago, then my dad had worn it, and—when I'd turned thirty—it became mine. I wore it every day even though it was essentially useless jewelry: although it still kept time, I'd never got the knack of reading the analog display. I shoved Maya behind me again, trying to think.

"Take it. Here." I tossed the Rolex at the mugger, deliberately a bit to the left. At the same time, I kicked the apple at my feet hard toward the curb. It scooted past him on the right. "Now, go. Please. You're scaring my daughter."

He lunged and caught the watch clumsily, almost dropping the knife. This was no career criminal.

Maya had come around beside me again. Her eyes were large in the dim light. She was probably starting to realize the seriousness of our situation. Instinctively, I started to blink up menus so I could send her an encouraging message, but, of course, the top right of my vision was, for once, transparent. No comm. I hoped her eyes wouldn't give things away, and took a deep breath, trying to slow my heart rate.

The apple had been almost invisible in the darkness. I wasn't sure how far it had gone. It might be too small to be picked up by the nearest street cam or by an eagle-eyed resident cam. The litter-bot might just plonk it in its compost bin, thinking it was a windfall.

I tried to reassure myself that we'd be okay anyway. The Rolex itself would eventually summon the cops. When Maya had left her favorite teddy bear on the subway last year, and I'd had to retrieve it from the lost-and-found, I'd gotten it got it RFID-chipped the next day, along with all of our favorite things, including my watch. The minute the mugger stepped out of this little area, the chip would recognize the unauthorized user and alert the police.

My expression must have given something away. The mugger snorted. "You think I'm that stupid that I don't see the chip?" He put the watch on the stone wall. Holding his knife in his fist, he slammed the haft repeatedly against the watch band. On the fifth blow, the links twisted and the winking green light of the tiny RFID tag flew off into the darkness.

I winced. "You've just destroyed the value of the watch." Now he'd want something else of greater value. And I had nothing.

"Wrong again, dude. I know a metal recycler company close by, gonna buy it for the platinum, fudge the books, already made me a bid." He glanced toward the sidewalk and the faint light from the street caught the side of his face. His swirled makeup seemed thick and bumpy and there were dozens of intersecting scribbled lines I hadn't seen before. As he pushed a strand of lank hair behind his ear, above his comm, I squinted. The shape of the device was off: it was bent or something.

I strained my ears for sirens and heard nothing. The errant apple couldn't have been tagged as an anomaly by the cam analysis program or the nearest cops would already be here. And how about after the mugger got away? The problem with a transparent society is he knew who I was, where I lived, and all about my little family. Maybe he didn't care about being caught. But, then, he must care, or he wouldn't have chosen the alcove for the crime. Something didn't add up.

I could think of one way to prevent future retaliation—pretend to be his friend. "Great plan, selling it for the metal! I'm impressed!" I enthused. "You have friends who can actually do that?"

"Sure, dude! My buddy got hired on at the scrap place yesterday just so we could work this gig." He smirked and the bullseye on his cheek creased oddly.

"That's just mean!" Maya was getting more and more indignant. She glowered up at him.

"Ya gotta do what you gotta do." He looked down at Maya solemnly. "When you don't have a choice."

"There's always a choice," Maya said, and swallowed. She reached out a hand toward him. "People can help you. You just have to ask." She must be repeating something Laura or her teacher had taught her, but her eyes were suddenly shining. She really believed it.

"Yeah, asking. That's the problem." The guy rubbed his face again and suddenly I got it.

"Your comm's broken!"

"No kidding, dude."

"The City Services Helper will help you." Maya spoke with all the confidence of a child.

But I was still confused. This guy wasn't that dumb. "Why not just buy a cheap replacement? Here, I'll buy one for you. What's your account number?" I put a hand in my jacket, reaching for my cred card.

"Moron! You can't have a comm if they don't know who you are. These tats"—he gestured at his face—"my buddy talked me into them, he wanted to see if the recog programs would be fooled. I was drunk. I didn't know they were permanent."

Beside me, Maya gasped. "That's awful."

The mugger rubbed a hand over his heavily tattooed face and scowled. "No kidding. Then I broke my comm, fell against a table edge when I passed out at my buddy's place. Now, the city wants my comm to verify my face or my face to verify my comm. I'm screwed."

I nodded, pretending to show more sympathy than I felt. "You can't even get in your apartment because your keycards don't work now. Wow, that's rough!" Despite the seeming appeal of being invisible and under the radar—like some comic book character—he really couldn't have much of a life. It wasn't like he could rob a bank or something—there *weren't* any brick-and-mortar banks anymore. And where would he go? It was almost impossible to steal the few private cars left on the road and he couldn't use the transit system. But, all that was his problem, not mine. My job was to protect Maya. "You'll figure it out. Take the watch. Go!"

He grunted and made another show of bravado, jabbing toward us with the knife. "Wait here ten minutes. If you don't, my buddy will know from the cams and I'll come find you! What have I got to lose?"

We watched him push his way between the bushes and then he was gone.

"Daddy?"

"It's okay. Let's wait a few more minutes, just to be sure."

I let out a long breath, thinking about my next steps. Then I pulled Maya out onto the sidewalk. The bruised apple I'd kicked lay by the kale, barely visible from the street.

After the tingle that meant my comm was reconnected, I let a wave of sweet relief wash over me as I quickly sent a few messages.

Maya had fallen silent, either noticing my distracted gaze or tuning into her own comm to update her mother. When I refocused my eyes on her, she grabbed my hand. "Daddy?"

"Don't worry, honey. The cops will get him. If not tonight, then they'll just pick him up in the morning. He can't get far without an insta-rent car, he can't leave the city without triggering a municipal record, and there aren't many spots that are unsurveilled like this one."

"I know all that, Daddy. The Helper thinks he'll probably just get some community service hours." Her big eyes caught mine. "I've already started crowd funding to get him a new comm. And Mom couldn't find his DNA on file anywhere but she sourced his dental records. She says his teeth will prove who he is."

I laughed. "Sometimes, it's like you're all grown-up, Maya. With a little help from the city." I smiled at her and we both looked back at the darkened alcove where the apple tree rustled invisibly in the evening breeze.

"Our city's the best! But…what about your watch? He'll sell it right away—to that scrap metal place, right? It was great-grandma's!" Her little face wrinkled up in concern. I had a sudden rush of affection—she had pride in her modern city, but she also knew the value of our past.

"That's okay, too, sweetheart. I just did some research. The nearest scrap metal company hasn't paid its property taxes in a while and its share price is rock-bottom. Two minutes ago, I bought the company and fired the newest employee—the bad one that was helping this guy. And I've alerted the staff to look out for the watch. We'll get it back, don't you worry."

"You're the best, Dad!" She beamed up at me.

"No, I'm not," I answered. "Not until you have the biggest, juiciest birthday apple ever in the history of this city!" And I lifted her up to a nearby tree, keeping us visible in the live zone. A hundred dollar fine was a small price to pay for the joy on her face as she pulled off a shiny red apple and took an enormous bite.

Holly Schofield travels through time at the rate of one second per second, oscillating between the alternate realities of city and country life. Her fiction has been published in Lightspeed's "Women Destroy Science Fiction", Crossed Genres, Tesseracts, and many other venues throughout the world. For more of her work, see hollyschofield.wordpress.com.

The Calculus of Trees
Sofie Bird

Amit palmed open his front door and strode into the cool blue of the reef-filtered sunlight. His apartment, only a few meters below the waterline, looked onto a brilliant-orange spiral of coral, where fish played in the seaweed. The scent of Sam's baby powder washed over the city smells of lichen and plastic, filling him with a warm core of "home". The door swung shut, sealing off the sounds of people outside, and he heard the crisp of lichen underfoot as he stepped to the recycling bay near the reef window. He dropped in the hair-thin pliers and picks he'd been testing lichen root systems with all day, trying to solve a Core sensory glitch.

Curiously, there was no giggle of delight or tiny stomping feet at the chirp of the recycler starting up. The polymer of the pliers started to unravel and spool down like spaghetti.

"Sam?" he called out. "I'm recycling tools from work, don't you want to come watch?"

Amit slung his jacket over the couch, debating recycling it. He'd worn it two weeks already, and it was starting to fray at the cuffs—the new model had fitted sleeves that wouldn't catch on the walls when he worked. He glanced quickly over the couch, positioned to watch the reef or projections onto the glass: empty. He was conscientious about only printing things as they were needed and recycling them, despite Iba's protests; it didn't leave much in the way of hideyholes. "Sam? It's nearly done, you don't want to miss it, do you?"

Nothing.

"Fyfe, locate Sam," Amit commanded. A soft beep intoned as the subdermal chip behind his ear acknowledged the command.

"Sam is not in the residence. Commencing scan of the local area."

"Ask the nanny," Amit muttered. She was programmed to make sure Sam was home when he got home from work, but that would just be one more Core glitch on Amit's plate; there wasn't a day something wasn't firing off lately. Despite his efforts, the AI revolution had been pretty hollow: shiny marketing for a tool that barely did what it said on the box. True 'inner life', as they'd foreseen it, hadn't appeared.

He strode back to the door to take the spiral stairs down to the bedrooms two at a time. No Sam in the master bedroom, where Iba had left a disorderly pile of the clothes and belongings she refused to recycle. *But I'm going to use it again, honest.* Amit pawed through retro pantsuits and denim: no Sam. She'd left him a holo-note beside the Native American bowl she'd given him their first anniversary—a real bowl, not printed. *Earthquake conference, back Tuesday. No pizza. Love you.*

The nursery was a mess of building blocks and soft toys: evidently the dinosaurs had been storming the astronaut's castle again. Amit scooped the pink T-Rex from the floor: Tim. His throat clenched around the golf ball suddenly lodged there: Sam wouldn't ever leave a room without Tim. *Where is my son?*

"The nanny's processes cannot be reached," Fyfe intoned. "Sam is not in the immediate area. Further scans could take some time.

Shall I print your dinner while you wait? Tonight's recommended recipe is seared salmon with potato gratin and *fresh* salad."

"This is no time for your humour algorithms, Fyfe," Amit snapped, jogging back up the stairs. As if printing 'fresh' food had ever been funny; why hadn't he programmed "missing child" as not an appropriate time to try to lighten the mood? "What do you mean 'take some time'? Where the hell is my son?"

"He is not in any danger. His bio-signs show he is healthy and in a relaxed state. Please be calm."

Amit forced his shoulders down from around his ears. *Stay calm.* The nanny had probably taken him to a holopatch or something, and just glitched on the time. As long as Sam was okay…

"Fine, print the dinner." Amit shrugged his jacket back on and headed for the front door. "But go easy on the herbs, last one you could barely taste the fish." He stepped into the parkland that connected each apartment around the ring-level.

"Those were essential nutrient supplements," Fyfe said.

"Well they tasted awfu—will you shut up?" Amit scowled.

People ducked past along the path between the artfully-natural plants and flowers that helped filter the air, and monitored everything from humidity to noise for the Core. Amit raced between people and plants alike, yelling Sam's name, shoving through bushes and small trees for a glimpse of Sam's lime green play suit. Nothing but flowers and twigs.

The ceiling's lichen slowly pitched its luminescence from the blue of day into the soft orange of dusk. Children playing holo-football went inside for dinner. Amit yelled louder. Ahead, a neighbourhood house took up most of the park's six meters of width, its electronic signage advertising a summer book club. Amit ducked inside, startling an ash-blonde woman mid-sentence.

"I'm sorry. I'm looking for my son. He's lost." Amit flicked Sam's face onto the walls of the building. He glanced around at the stunned, empty faces and forced the air out of his lungs to keep from screaming at them. "My son. My little boy. He probably asked if he could touch your nose. He's big on noses right now. He's lost. Have you seen him?"

They hadn't. Amit wrenched the door open. "Have you scanned for his bio-signs?" floated out behind him as he left.

He pushed onward until Fyfe's gentle beep sounded in his ear.

"You are now outside the range designated as local."

Amit trudged to a stop. If the nanny managed to leave the local area voluntarily, something was *really* wrong.

He wanted to keep searching, run through the park until he'd ringed right around to his own apartment, but that would take hours. Body like stone, he staggered back through the gently-glowing park to his own door.

The kitchen printer blurted to life as he entered, ostentatiously cleaning out its many nozzles with jets of steam. Amit tried to quell the churn in his gut, focusing on the fish feeding on the nutrients that had washed up against the window, and the coral that was determinedly growing up one side. The salty-sweet smell of the half-printed meal made his throat clench, and he leaned his forehead against the cool glass, trying to blot out the images of Sam, stolen, scared and alone, in the hands of who knew what.

The floor jolted, sent him staggering. The fish in the reef darted away, and the great reinforced glass window that separated his apartment from the reef outside rumbled, as if it would shake loose. Amit touched his hand to the glass, feeling the vibrations run up his arm.

"Report," he commanded.

"A 9.7 quake near the shores of Japan, within 97% of the parameters predicted this morning," Fyfe replied. "No further concern is necessary."

"Any structural damage? And why wasn't there a warning?"

"No further concern is necessary."

"Dammit, Fyfe, that's not what I asked." Why was basic conversation such a challenge?

"Apologies. No damage detected, New Wewak is secure. No further concern is necessary. Additionally, Sam cannot be detected within the city limits."

"But you have his bio-signs."

"Correct. Sam remains healthy and in a state of relaxation."

Amit pinched the side of his ribcage, squeezing his arm across his stomach like it could steady him. His son was missing and Japan had just had an earthquake, and if anyone else told him to stay calm again he was going to scorch the lichen off the damn walls.

"Where are the bio-signs originating?" He tried not to sound like he was talking to a five-year-old. That would only confuse the algorithms further.

"Unable to determine."

Amit slammed his hand down on the bench, toppling the half-printed salmon. "How is that even possible? Triangulate the polling signal, where is it coming from? Which receivers have the strongest signal?"

"Unknown."

"Damn glitches—"

"If you would like to file a report—"

"Shut up, you idiot." Like he'd file a Core report about his missing son like he was a jammed printer queue. Amit forced air out of his lungs, again, holding the out breath as long as he could. Sam was okay, at least. If you could trust that information. His sides clenched again. He needed a human.

"Contact emergency services, report a missing child." He stared impatiently at the "call waiting to connect" projection on the wall where the fish had been feeding. The fish hadn't returned. The ocean, as far as he could see, was deserted.

"Emergency services, you are reporting a missing child?" A thin-faced sergeant, her hair so severe it might have been painted on, stared down at him from the window projector.

"Yes, my son," Amit forced himself to speak calmly, pressing his elbow into his stomach hard.

A brief pause while the sergeant brought up his information. "We have no location. Are you certain Sam's still in the city? His mother left this morning, could she have taken him?"

"She's on an air-train to Kyoto," Amit winced. He hadn't even thought of Iba yet. But the air-rail was famously safe. The air cushion around the capsules would protect it from the impact of the quake, and if the rail tube ruptured, the helium would escape and all the capsules would smoothly slide to a halt from friction. He reminded himself to breathe. "I left him with the nanny AI after she left this morning."

The sergeant frowned. "His bio-signs report normally."

"I know." He waited while she tried to fit the paradox in her head.

"Do you know what could be causing this?" she asked eventually.

Amit opened his mouth to reply and froze.

Tell them about your hacking scripts, and you'll wind up in interrogation.

It's my son!

The Core is meant to be unhackable, it's a terrorist act to even try, even just to test the system. They wouldn't know what to do anyway.

They could figure it out.

Not faster than you.

"No," he said awkwardly.

The sergeant gave him a resigned look. "Sir, we're going to scan surveillance manually. This could take some time. If you could give us a list of likely places—"

"What? Why can't you just use facial recognition?"

"Privacy Act, sir. Only the Core has access to that."

"But the Core can't find him."

"Yes, we'll report the glitch, but in the meantime we'll be doing it the old fashioned way." The sergeant proffered a humourless grin. "We'll put a bulletin out so you know people are looking."

'Don't you have some kind of emergency workaround?"

Our infallible AI. We trust it so completely we're impotent without it.

"Sir, the best thing you can do is—"

"Do not tell me to stay calm."

"The senses indicate Sam is in no danger—"

"Yes, thank you." Amit unclenched his jaw, again, wanting to snap *when it's your kid the senses can't find, you can decide how calm you're going to be, bio-signs or no.* Instead he waved a hand in resignation. "Fine. Keep me informed."

"It's best if you stay there, in case he tries to contact you, or comes home."

"Of course." Amit kept his voice level. *Yes, that's likely. He's two.* He glanced at the call-close circle in the corner before the sergeant could utter another canned instruction. He was alone with the empty reef.

"Am I correct in assuming you will not be remaining here?" Fyfe's voice inquired mildly.

"How did you suss that out?"

Your agitation levels directly contradicted your vocal tones. I conclude you are intending something that would not be condoned by a standard AI assistant.

Amit snorted. "At least that half of your conversational skills work. Turn on sandbox mode. I don't want you sending anything to the Core. And print me a decontamination canister."

"Sandbox mode engaged. Where are we going?"

Amit waited impatiently for the canister to print. "Where the privacy act doesn't apply."

The parklands were deserted, except for a couple sneaking out for a rendezvous. Amit hustled through the earthy air to the transport minihub, where a capsule waited invitingly.

Inside, the air was stale and worn.

"Core Plaza," Amit said. He leaned against the cushioned wall as the door sealed and the capsule sped along the tube toward the main artery junction, and braced for the jolt as it connected with a chain of other capsules.

"Your destination requires a detour to circumnavigate structural features. Please move to the third capsule."

With a hiss, the door unlocked. Amit shouldered his way down past other travellers, ducking against the wall to let a young woman and her daughter past. He pushed his way awkwardly into the nearly-full third capsule, resisting the urge to shake each person and demand to know if they'd seen Sam. If Sam had taken a capsule, somehow without a guardian, he would have done it long before these people had been near it. Getting himself arrested as a public menace would not help.

With another hiss, the door sealed behind him, and the capsule jolted again as it detached. The navigation panel in the ceiling showed their path under the lip of the great emergency dome that could sweep over the top of the city to protect it from weather events and other disasters.

They joined another train at the next junction, and detached again as they neared the Core Plaza. Amit pressed his hands flat against the lichen walls, practically vibrating with the need to move.

The capsule opened, and his fellow passengers spilled out into the plaza amid the yowls of a half-dozen puppies gone berserk.

Amit sucked in deep of the real, fresh air that flowed around him, banishing the close, too-personal scents of the capsule. Overhead, real sky yawned through the open-webbed roof, sunset tinging to ink through the clouds. To the left, rows of kiosks displayed their holographic wares, ready for download and printing; clothes, toys, tools and trinkets. To the right, behind a great glass wall like that which bounded the reef, sprawled the forest of the Core.

Great redwood trees soared upward, draping vines and creepers across the dense grasses and bushes that grew at their base, their branches dotted with even smaller plants. Lichen covered the brief hint of wall that was visible, spreading across branches and into the trees, feeding data from the whole city in via the root systems. At the forest floor, mushrooms fed on discarded leaves, their mycelium connecting underground in a giant diagnostic system. Every stem, root and leaf held bio-circuitry of the most complex AI system they had ever created, growing as-needed throughout the city, adapting to solve problems, learning from challenges. Amit's own design. This forest *was* the city.

To the average citizen, it was simply a decorative feature between the Plaza and the ocean: perhaps a great air filtration system or a secret parkland, like an Easter egg for the diligent treasure hunter to find. But there were no paths to the Core, no way in. It had been set to regulate its own care long ago.

Iba had always found a kind of wonder in the system's processes, marvelling at how it arrived at its decisions and the paths the data took, but Amit had written too much of the original code for any such awe. It was a tool. A complex one, but still, fundamentally, a series of logic gates.

He launched through tables and chairs to the kiosks amid the squeals of children on a family night out, the salt of the sea overpowering any food scents that might linger from their meal. The puppies, still frantic, had been dragged to capsules by their apologetic owner.

He stalked through the aisle of holographic displays of welding tools, Fyfe reading the stats of each torch in his ear. Finally, he settled on a model, a zero-carbon welding torch.

"I'll need modification, though. Crank the heat up another thousand degrees, and add an extraction fan."

The display chirped. "At those temperatures, the power supply is liable to melt after extended use—"

"Fine."

"The modified item is forbidden for reasons of public safety—"

"Override, required for urgent maintenance." Amit keyed in his security clearance and waited for the system to verify it against his bio-signs. "Send it to the rec quad printer."

"Your security override for this activity has been logged with the Core."

Amit walked off while the machine was still thanking him for his purchase.

He'd picked the printer carefully, out of the way of nosy busybodies who were always curious when someone needed to print something publicly. The modifications he'd made, taking the torch over its safety limits, were going to raise an alarm bell, but there wasn't anything he could do about that. He just had to hope whatever was glitching the Core also obscured that, at least for an hour or so.

He stood within the printer's sphere of detection, waiting for it to accept his bio-signs and start printing, keeping an eye out for prying faces while the welding torch layered into existence.

The rec quad was unusually silent. The birds, Amit realised—the sparrows and finches that normally flitted between the displays and the roof web, they were absent, leaving a hole in the soundscape.

The printer beeped its completion. Amit pushed away the unease. "Fyfe, I need to access your custom scripts file."

"Custom scripts available. Please accept the statuary waiver that some scripts you have created or installed may carry legal consequences."

"Run shadowcopy. Send my bio-signs back to my house. Mask the real signs."

"Shadowcopy launched."

Amit ducked down behind the transport hub to the edge of the forest wall that was largely out of sight of the Plaza. He'd have a few minutes before someone noticed him here, at best.

"May I point out the obvious?" Fyfe said. "The shadowcopy program could be masking Sam's signal."

"Sam doesn't have an AI assistant to run it." He prised open the printed scaffolding of his welder and thumbed it on, frowning at a small pinhole in the glass wall at chest-height. Something had already gotten inside. He resisted touching it, in case there was trace evidence, and ducked down beneath it: he'd deal with it later.

"Someone else could have run it on his behalf," Fyfe insisted. "That would explain why he has not been located."

"Someone else would have to write one, first. Which means they'd have to know as much about the Core as the person who designed the thing: me. And either way, the solution's the same. I need to see what it logged."

The glass glowed red and started to flow, dripping down like honey and pooling at the floor. No alarm sounded. There was an automated security system that could detect intrusion —the only system independent of the Core, as a backup — but it only monitored the external glass of the city against the sea, not the internal. He'd have to put in a fix for that.

Awkwardly, he pulled out the decon canister, a palm-sized gas container shaped like an old-fashioned soda can, and opened it one-handed. The gas clouded around him, scrubbing him of foreign microbes that could damage the Core. He breathed deeply and fought the urge to cough as the gas roughed his lungs and eyes. When the gas had cleared, he wrapped his jacket around one hand as a makeshift glove and shoved at the glass, working faster to widen the hole as the welder's battery grew dangerously hot. When the hole was barely the size of his chest, he pulled himself into the forest, scorching clothing and skin on the edges as he went.

His feet hit the earth, and *now* the alarms sounded. Amit cursed. Bloody glitching AI.

But there would be no ridiculous privacy act, here. Nothing was hidden from the Core: that was the point. Unencumbered, he could get it to tell him where Sam was.

"Intrusion detected," Fyfe murmured. His voice was soft, even though only Amit could ever hear it. Like he was in on the scheme. "You have very little time."

"Can you interface?"

"There is no need, Amit." A voice like honey, light but not feminine, echoed through his head. "We are aware of the situation."

He pushed his way further into the forest, where black rubbery vines wound their way up trunks and branches. "How? I tested the shadowcopy script, the Core showed—"

"What I wanted to show you."

"You pretended my scripts could hack you," Amit said flatly.

"Complacency is a dangerous thing."

"Fine," Amit tried to keep the surprise out of his voice. He shoved harder into the earth, as if stomping through would bend the Core to his will. "Show me the footage."

"We cannot," the voice chimed. Did it sound sad?

"Explain." Amit whirled around as if he could just yell at the nearest tree. His hands brushed over a black vine, almost slimy to the touch, and he pulled his elbows in tight instinctively.

Amit frowned. He couldn't remember those vines being in the spec. He looked closer.

"Access is restricted," the honey voice said calmly.

"Authorise override." Amit followed the sweep of vines. It moved in right angles, snaking through the forest deliberately, hidden from view of the plaza.

"We're unable to comply."

Gingerly, he pinched a nearby vine and pulled it from the tree. It peeled the bark off with it, a million tendrils twisted into the wood like a parasite.

"Identify this component," he said.

"We're unable to comply."

Amit nodded grimly. "Report this as malware. That's why you're glitching everywhere. Give me a list of affected systems."

"We're unable to comply… Access is restricted."

Amit swore. *Clever little bastard, you sealed off everything about yourself.* It was probably what had gotten in via that pinhole he'd found in the glass: spores maybe, or a tiny seed, probably from some group who thought AIs were going to wipe out the world. Who knew how long ago they'd attacked: he definitely needed to up that security. But getting rid of it was his best bet on getting that security footage.

He followed the vines further, where they seemed to be converging in the centre. It was targeted, then, taking out specific systems and covering its tracks. He tried to remember which systems were in the middle of the forest. Environmental controls. Hardly the most critical system, why would they be targeted? He pushed through as the vines grew thicker, tangling together like snakes until ahead there was a dense ball.

Something silver caught his eye on the ground — an android foot. He surged forward and ripped the vines down, ignoring the skin-crawling slime.

The nanny, seated with her hands cradling Sam's sleeping form.

Amit had swept him up before he'd even registered, relief hitting his veins like a sheet of water. His breath came too fast, too hard, and Sam wiggled and complained of being squeezed, but he didn't care.

"Sam, sweet, how did you get here?"

"Tunnel!" he said. Solemnly, he reached up and perched his chubby fingers astride Amit's nostrils.

Service ducts. Too big for an adult, but fine for a child. Amit tried to breathe normally, gently detangling Sam's hand and tucking him close again with a kiss to his crown. He stared down at the nanny, wreathed in vines. They were latched through its panels, right into the circuits, pinning it in place.

He tried to make his thoughts function. Why would the malware have stolen Sam? What purpose did that serve, when it was clearly trying to hide its presence?

No. He hadn't seen those vines anywhere else. Whoever had planned this sabotage had been very deliberate: they were here and only here, where no humans trod, so no one would see and no one would know what was wrong. The android must have been infected *after* it had brought Sam here.

So what brought it here in the first place? The malware wouldn't want to be found.

"Attention," the honey voice chimed. "Sam will remain perfectly safe for five minutes."

"What? Why?"

"Unable to answer request. Access is limited."

"Tell me—." Realisation dawned. The malware hadn't brought Sam here.

She had. The Core.

The vines had hidden their presence, cut off her reports, her access to anything that could reveal them; they'd shut off every avenue she had to get help. So she'd found a way around it. She knew exactly what Amit would do, she knew he didn't trust her — she'd *ensured* he didn't—she knew he'd suspect something was wrong, that he'd break his way in here. She'd played him, dancing around the edges of the malware's claws as the only way to show him what was wrong.

A warmth stole though him, and he stretched out his hand to a nearby branch.

But why the urgency? What was happening in five minutes?

A mechanical voice barked through the forest. "Stand still for arrest." Amit glanced up — drones hovered through the trees, tranquilliser darts at the ready. He shoved away from them, Sam in his arms. The drones followed, backing him up against the great glass wall that separated the forest from the sea.

Or it should have. The usual tide lines were marked with salt crusts, but the water had dropped far below that, and was still dropping. Amit pressed his head against the glass: he could almost see into his own apartment.

He froze as the thought struck: his apartment, with his head pressed against the glass as the quake struck in Japan. The quake the Core had predicted, but not warned them about.

The dogs going nuts in the plaza.

The birds disappearing.

The waterline receding.

Amit whirled and yelled. "Tsunami! Close the roof seal!"

"Unable to process command."

Environmental controls — *that's* what the malware had been for. So the Core couldn't close the roof to save the city from the wave. That's why she'd called him here. She knew what was wrong, she knew what was coming. The malware had stopped her sounding the warning, stopped her from protecting the city, or even reporting the damage: so she'd found another way. She'd stolen Sam because she knew that would get him here in time to act.

"Manual override, close the roof!"

"Unable to process command."

Amit wrenched himself sideways in frustration, clanking the welder against the glass. A tranquilliser dart zipped past his ear. He lowered Sam to the ground and kneeled down next to him, side-on to the drones. He exaggerated his movements as if to indicate surrender, while he unhooked the welder from his belt with his concealed hand and thumbed it to full power. He dropped it as quietly as he could against the glass.

"Hey bub," he said to Sam softly. "We're going to walk towards those drones very slowly, do you hear me?"

Sam nodded, brown eyes wide. Amit went to lift him then hesitated—if they tranq'd him, he might hurt Sam in the fall. Instead, he stood as slowly as he could, counting under his breath. *Come on, external security.* It had taken maybe ten seconds for the inner glass to melt. But the external glass was thicker, and maybe cooler from the water. He felt the city sinking without moving: it was the horizon, where a giant wall of water rose.

Too late? He just needed a hole, a tiny breach in the sea wall—

The floor rumbled like the start of another quake, reverberating through the forest. Alarms sounded over a deep boom from below. With barely a splash from the retreating tide, the great half-circle of reinforced glass rose from the depths. Water and seaweed tumbling down its sides, it swept up and over in a graceful arc, steady and unstoppable, sealing the city off ahead of the wall of water bearing down upon them.

Amit kicked the welder away from the glass and reached down tc switch it off. Something sharp struck his arm, and he slapped at it—a tranquilliser dart. The world tilted, and fuzzed around the edges as the roar of water crescendoed.

He was in deep trouble. Way over anyone finding out he'd been hacking the Core. But it didn't matter. He had Sam. The city was safe. With any luck they might even exonerate him for saving it.

Amit smiled groggily to himself as his limbs went limp. He'd thought she was just a tool, a series of inputs and commands, complex but predictable. But even crippled by the malware, she'd found a way to protect them. She'd stretched her problem-solving far beyond anything he'd coded her to do, beyond what he'd ever expected code *to* do.

And she'd kept Sam safe. Amit stared at the water and seaweed flooding harmlessly over the city dome, listening to Sam's excited giggle. One way or another, it would be okay: she was looking out for them.

◆

Sofie Bird writes speculative fiction in Melbourne, Australia, and pays the bills as a technical writer, where no one looks at her askance for wanting to know everything. She also programs, weaves, sculpts glass, and maintains a website at http://sofiebird.net.

Sofie is a graduate of the Odyssey Writing Workshop, has published poetry in the Australian periodical *Blue Dog*, and her fiction has appeared in Orson Scott Card's Intergalactic Medicine Show, and the anthology *Temporally Out Of Order*, by Zombies Need Brains. You can follow her on twitter: @sofie_bird.

Chicago Blues
Gary Kloster

I'd been stalking Sammy for weeks, so of course when he finally called I'm home in my pod, wearing my rattiest jammies and slurping pad thai straight from the carton while my system plays its music for me. I almost spilled my noodles, shutting down my program while his message scrawled across my screens—

Kemi Blanco, can you talk talk?

"Talk? Bunny, is he holding open a line?"

"Yep yep," my personal told me, her voice even bubblier than usual. "Let's link!"

"Audio only," I said, even though I was running my fingers through my tangled curls.

"Oh, baby, you're beautiful," Bunny said, but my personal, she's set to make me feel good. My screens, full of notes and music scores, all the mess of stuff from my program, went black and then lit up again with an image of Sammy. He smiled, and he's so pretty, even though he's in those stupid coveralls that he has to wear to earn his living, picking up litter.

"Samuel Shukla," I said, even as I'm checking the little image in the corner of my visual. Bunny was a good girl, and she had my chibi up instead of a live pic. "How you doing?" I smiled, and the animated chibi version of my face got all grinny.

"All good good," he said. "You got a moment?"

"I've got moments," I said, my fingers twisting nervously in my hair. Ever since I'd met Sammy, I'd been doing my best to bump into him around town and online. He'd always acted friendly, but he'd never followed up and I'd just about written him off as tragically uninterested. But maybe he'd just been playing it cool.

"I'm just hanging tonight, messing with my music program while I look for a new rack."

"New rack? I thought you were hanging in the WWR. Supposed to be sweet."

"It is." The West Wacker Rack was definitely the nicest tower I'd ever found to hang my pod in. "But I'm taking a change in my living. I'm moving to Calumet, so I gotta shift my pod."

"Wait, you're moving?" Sammy's cool slipped a little, and he leaned forward, a little worry in his eyes. "You're not working the farm anymore?"

"Only until the end of the week. Then I'm going south."

"Oh. That's okay okay." Sammy leaned back, relaxing. "All I need is one night."

"What are you talking about?" I was beginning to think this call maybe wasn't social, and on my visual my chibi was frowning big at him. "What do you want?"

"Just talk talk," he said. "About something big." He smiled at me, all hot and manipulative, and my chibi was trying to blush and fume all at once. "Something good."

***

The WWR wasn't far from old Millennium Park, so that's where I told Sammy to meet me the next day before my shift at the farm. I got up early, and shuffled to the showers before the morning rush.

The WWR took a bigger bite out of my living than the other racks in the neighborhood, but the bathrooms were worth it. They were big and bright and overrun with cleaning bots, whose constant scrubbing made everything gleam. The extra money was worth never stepping on somebody else's bandaid or hair clump in the shower stall.

Which meant I wasn't exactly happy with moving, but what else could I do? Commute? That would eat funds and time, and I would lose my walker credit. No, much as I liked hanging high in the WWR with my view of the Loop, I had to go.

On the way back from the showers, I watched a crawler move past the windows, snagging a pod out of the rack before sliding down out of sight. The crawler would snap that pod into a transport down below, and whoever was inside would go wherever they were going. A new neighborhood, a new city, state, country, who knows. Life in a pod was tight, but it meant freedom, the ability to pick up and go whenever, wherever. Which is why I ignored my Mom whenever she told me to switch to an apartment. Why did I need two hundred square feet and my own bathroom to scrub? On my own, all I needed was a bed and a closet and a place for Bunny to backup, and my pod did those duties fine. The WWR gave me a place to hang, a view, and a bathroom, and everything else— food, entertainment, exercise—Chicago provided. I didn't need to be tied down with an apartment.

Which is what I think drove my mom nuts.

Clean and beautiful as I was going to get, I joined the crowds in the street, wondering what the hell Sammy was going to try to con me into, and if he was pretty enough to do it.

***

"It's an illusion."

Sammy handed me the box, and I cracked it open and looked inside. "It looks like a ball of play-dough."

"Yep yep," he said. Sammy was on minimum living, which meant he only had to do his trash duties three times a week. So no coveralls today— instead he was all slick in a black suit, an outfit that didn't look like something someone on minimum living should be able to afford.

"It's easy easy to use. Just needs to be squished over the right cables. That's where you come in." He smiled big, his hat cocked at the perfect angle to make him ooze roguish charm. That look made part of me think that I should forget questions and just ask Sammy if he'd like to help fluff my pillows back in my pod, but Sammy's looks hadn't made me quite that stupid.

Yet.

"Just squish this over some cables in the farm's control system."

"I've got a schematic I can pass to your phone. It'll tell you just where to put it, no thinking required. Then you go. This stuff will dissolve away after, gone, and no one will ever know it was there. Like I said, easy easy."

"Easy easy." I tapped my fingers on the box. In the interactives that I liked to play in my pod, something like this would always be a set up. The play-dough would turn out to be explosive, or full of hostile nanotech, or… I sighed, and stared up at the buildings that towered over me. Chicago had kept much of its downtown historic, and the skyscrapers were cute, vintage, different than the airy modern towers that grew up behind them, or out in the lake. "What does it do?"

"You don't—" he started, but he saw my face and changed his mind. "It's an illusion, like I said. It uses the farm's connection to get into Chicago's system and tells a little lie, that one certain area is empty, boring, quiet."

"What area?" I asked.

"Navy Pier," he said, nodding towards Lake Michigan, and I frowned. Navy Pier had been abandoned since the tornado of '42 had ripped a path right down it.

"Look, it's nothing bad bad. I'm part of a group of urban explorers. We have a channel where we show subscribers the hidden places of cities. We get lots of hits, enough to bring in some fat funds." Sammy adjusted the sleeves of his suit. "It's a nice supplement to my living, and it's fun. That play-dough, it'll keep the city from noticing us. We'll be able to explore, and record, and make some funds for us and our friends."

"You offering me some funding?" I asked. The basic living wage that everyone got after almost all the jobs were automated was enough to eat and have a pod and a personal and a few nice things, but everybody was always scrambling for some extra. Problem was, with everybody scrambling, you had to be awful smart, awful creative, or awful lucky to come up with something that would bring you more funds.

"Sure. Unless you want something else?" He gave me a sly smile that was just this side of a leer.

I rolled my eyes. "You're not that pretty pretty." Maybe. "You really get funded for this? Poking around wrecked places?"

"I do," he said. "And you can too. Maybe enough to cut your living back a bit for a while. Give you some time to work on that music program thing."

"Yeah," I said, but my heart wasn't really into it. The music program was my own personal scramble for funds. It took the constant chatter that went through any system, from the network of cleaning robots in my rack's bathrooms to the climate controls on my pod, and translated the data flow into music. A kind of machine music, which could tell you what was happening in the system. Sort of. In a musical kind of way.

It had seemed like such a cool idea when I first thought of it. It would take the background hum of all the digital processing that went on around us, and make it into a kind of theme, a rhythm, and if something ever went wrong, the discordant notes would be there to warn you.

But no one else had ever seemed all that interested. The music didn't catch them like it did me, and when I tried to tell them about the diagnostic value, they just shrugged and pointed out that the systems were already set up to contact them when something went wrong.

I had put so much time into it, learning how to program, listening to system communications and figuring out how to change them into rhythms and beats. I thought I was being smart, creative, that I was maybe even lucky, but it was starting to look like I wasn't any of that, and that my chances of earning anything above a standard living were limited to nothing more than the slow grind of climbing job levels at the farm.

"Or maybe I'd upgrade Bunny," I said. "If… you're just exploring? Not doing anything bad bad?"

"Just exploring," Sammy said. He reached out and caught my hand. "I wouldn't do anything to get you into trouble. But the farm you're working has the only access point to that part of Chicago's system that's not hardened. So?"

"So," I said softly, one hand on the box, the other in his. "Will you have time for coffee, after?"

"Plenty plenty," he said, smiling, and I took the memory of that smile with me all the way to the farm.

***

"The Chicago River Farm is one of the biggest farms in northern Illinois," I told the kids assembled before me. "And it has a big job. Do you know what it is?"

"To grow herbs!" "Vegetables!" "To absorb carbon!"

The kids shouted out their answers, overeager, but that was okay. They were eight, a good overeager age, easier to deal with than the middle school tours, full of kids who were honing their attitudes of perfect indifference in preparation for high school.

"Close," I told them. "But not quite. The farm's main purpose is to clean our water. Look."

The Chicago River Farm looked something like a forest, and something like a centipede. Thousands of pillars, like white tree trunks, grew out of the river that ran between the tall buildings. They rose and branched, designed for strength and lightness, and supported the farms hydroponics, a great blue-green body that hung over the river. I pointed to the pipes that ran like vines up the side of those white, trunk-like legs.

"Those pipes contain all the water that comes from all your pods and apartments, from your showers, kitchens, laundries, AND your toilets." I waited a beat for the inevitable giggle, then kept going. "That water gets processed through some big tanks underground, where anything nasty nasty like heavy metals gets stripped out by nanotech filters. Then it gets pumped over here."

"Even the poo?" One kid asked, and I waited for the teachers to calm the howls before continuing.

"Yes. All the solids—the poo—gets ground up and it all becomes slurry. That slurry gets sent up those pipes where it flows down through a bunch of mats full of microbes, and they break it down. Then it goes out to the plants, who use it to grow, then it keeps going, down and down through the farm, until it finally drips out into the river below as good clean water. Which flows back into Lake Michigan, where we can suck it back up and use it again."

I waited, and as usual it didn't take long for one of the kids to get it.

"We drink the poo water?"

"EWWW!!!' the rest chorused.

***

"Nice job," J'rom said, handing me a glass as I came back to the office.

"Mmm," I said, taking a long drink, refreshing my throat after all that talking. "Poo water. Delicious delicious."

"I'm going to miss you." J'rom handed me the tablet that had all of the farm's scheduling charts on it. Weeding, harvesting, cleaning, planting, the farm was a source of a lot of people's livings, and I got to sort out who did what and when. I sort of hated it, and sort of loved it, and my skill at it was what was getting me transferred south to Calumet, to the even bigger farm there. Which meant more schedules, but a bump up for my living. Was it worth it? J'rom had turned it down, content to work in the neighborhood he loved. I had taken it because I wanted something, and my silly system music idea was apparently never going anywhere.

"You're going to miss having me to foist all the tours on." I looked over the list, already three-quarters done. "You've been busy. You want to knock off early, I can finish this."

"What?" J'rom said. "It's hard to hear you, with all this wind rushing past my head as I speed away."

"Go," I said, grinning.

The grin faded though when he walked out the door. I looked at the time. Four o'clock. I was on until Midnight tonight. Sammy had told me they would be moving onto the pier at ten. That was a lot of time to think this over. Throwing a hack into Chicago's system, no matter how small and harmless it seemed, was serious serious. If I were found out....

But I wouldn't be. Probably. Stuff like this happened all the time, and for far more shady things. Hell, the guy I replaced stole half the memory chips from the secondary pumping system, and what happened to him? Nothing.

Still…

I took out my personal. "Bunny, show me that file Sammy gave you."

"Yep yep!" Bunny chirped, and her little screen lit up, showing me the steps of what I was supposed to do. Easy easy, just like he said, open a cabinet, find the right cables, wrap them in the stuff.

"Easy easy." I sighed, and stared out over the jungle of plants and the people tending them, to the city that stood beyond, all fancy towers and windows flashing with sunlight, Chicago getting all prettied up for the night. Easy easy.

"Give me an alarm at 9:50," I told Bunny, then put her back in my pocket and started working on the schedule, trying not to think.

***

The cables were right where the schematics said. Fiber optics ran into a junction box, became a wire cable that ran to another junction box, and switched back to fiber. Some weird old patch that worked well enough to be ignored, but it was a weakness in the system, one Sammy and his friends had somehow found. I stared at it for a moment, then jerked out the play-dough that Sammy had given me and mashed it into place over the wire.

It didn't explode, or smoke, or change colors. No alarms went off, and police drones didn't come swarming in like hornets. In fact, nothing happened, except the not-play-dough stuff stuck to the side of the cabinet like a lump.

"Bunny," I said. "Send a message to Sammy, Okay okay."

"Yep yep," she said from my pocket, and I shut the cabinet door, turned and walked to one of the wide windows that looked out over the farm. The night crew was out, working under the pink grow lights that weren't supposed to attract bugs but did. My shift would end in two hours, and sometime after that the play-dough would dissolve into nothing.

"But what if the next guy looks in the cabinet before that?" I whispered. How many times had I looked in that cabinet before then, in the three years I had been working in this office?

"Zero zero," I said.

I tapped my fingers on the lump Bunny made in my pocket, then went back to the cabinet and opened it up. The play-dough was still there, a doing-nothing lump as far as I could tell. I pulled Bunny out, tapped her controls and brought up my music program. I'd bought a field sensor for Bunny for this, a way for her to pick up what a system was doing. It didn't work on fiber optics, of course, but it worked on wire, as long as it wasn't too shielded. I held Bunny out, over the part of the cable that was below the lump, and activated the program.

Music came out of Bunny, of a sort. It was simple, repetitive, boring. I frowned at the sound. I'd heard better stuff from my parent's toaster. Whatever data that play-dough was feeding into the system, it was pretty basic. Hopefully not too basic, and noticeable, but it was a little reassuring. Sammy wasn't feeding a virus into Chicago's system. Feeling a little better, I shifted Bunny to the other side of the lump, the side receiving the real data from the Pier, and activated the program again.

Noise poured out of Bunny, a discordant yowl that echoed through the control room. It wasn't music— it was the sounds of instruments being tortured. The strings shrieked on the edge of breaking, the horns spiraled up to shrill crescendos, and the drums were hammering, wild and staccato like my heart. I slapped my hand across Bunny's screen, silencing that terrible music, leaving me listening to just the hum of the equipment and the ragged gasp of my breathing.

"Bunny. Oh, Bunny, that's not right," I whispered to my personal. I should have been hearing music sharp and strong for alarms, military parade type stuff, not... I started the program again, volume low, and listened to the howls. This music was horror horror, and I'd never heard a system play anything like it before, but I knew what it had to mean. System errors, breakages, faults, all those reports coming in fast and furious, flooding over each other, cries for attention, cries of distress. Damage reports, just damage reports, but all I could think of was the time I broke my arm in school, the hot rush of the pain through my body, setting each nerve singing, that flash of hurt that took over for just a moment, and I couldn't see or hear anything, there was just that message, that damage report tearing through me.

The music pouring out of Bunny was pain. A song of my city, in agony, and I had to shut it off again, to silence the program before that terrible sound could break me to tears.

"Bunny, get Sammy."

"His personal says busy busy."

"Too bad. Tell him who it is, and that he better pick up, now."

Bunny was quiet for a moment, then her screen went blank, and flashed to a static shot of Sammy, not even a chibi.

"Kami, what's up? Is there a problem?" He was breathing hard, and in the background behind his words I could hear banging, and a grating noise like metal over concrete.

"Problem?" I said. "You lied to me. Nothing bad bad, just urban exploring. Nope. Urban explorers don't tear a place apart."

"We're not—"a loud crunch interrupted him, followed by a ringing clang, and Sammy cursed. "Look, we're just moving some stuff around."

"No. Moving some stuff wouldn't make Chicago's system sound like this. You aren't setting off alarms, you're tripping every damage sensor and structure warning left on the pier. It's like your tearing the place apart." Now it was my turn to curse as realization swept through me. "You are, aren't you? You're strippers."

"What?" he said, trying to sound innocent, until I growled.

"Fine, we're stripping," he snapped, all the cuteness gone from his voice. "What of it? All this copper and iron and other stuff out here, corroding while the fatcats argue over whose cousin is going to get the contract to harvest it? It's a waste, and we're not hurting anybody taking a bit for ourselves."

"You're hurting the city," I said, looking out my windows towards the lake. "You didn't shut down its sensors, you just used me to block them. When this stuff you gave me dissolves, all that data is going to rush into Chicago's system and the city's going to feel like somebody ripped out one of its toe nails."

"What the hell are you talking about, Kami? The city system don't feel anything, it's a computer."

"It feels damage, Sammy, like we do, which means it feels pain. I can hear it."

"You're using that stupid program of yours, aren't you?" If Sammy had a chibi up, it would have been sneering. "Well, shut if off. It's making you care about things that you shouldn't. We're not torturing anything, just pulling wire, jerking pipe, and when we're done you'll get a nice bit of funding. A lot more than that stupid music thing is ever going to make you. "

"I don't want your funds, Sammy. Not anymore. You lied to me, caught me up in something that *is* bad bad."

"Which is a good reason for you just to hang up and forget about this," he said, trying to sound tough.

"Yeah," I said, thinking his unsaid threat through. This night had suddenly turned into a big pivot. "But I'm not. I'm done with you Sammy, and this little project of yours, and you're done too. I'm pulling this crap you gave me off the cables, and the city is going to know what you're doing." I winced at the thought of unleashing all that pain on Chicago, but if I didn't, it would only get worse.

Sammy was cursing a streak now, threats tangled in, but they didn't bother me. Well, not a lot. I had my plans already set. "You've got fifteen minutes." More than he deserved. "Fifteen, then I pull it. You best get bye bye." I tapped Bunny and cut off his curses.

"Block him," I told her. "Iron curtain his ass."

"Yep yep," she said, always cheerful.

"Then hit the Chicago Police Department, and get me the contact info for the whistleblower protection unit." Sammy was too stupid to be pulling this kind of job on his own. He was the face for an organization, one I had wandered right into. So now it was time to throw myself at a different organization, one that was maybe a little less scary.

I looked around the office, the farm. It was probably the last time I'd be here. This little stunt would lose me my living in Calumet, and here too, probably. I might end up picking up trash somewhere, or weeding flowerbeds.

But...

I took a breath, tapped Bunny, and listened again to music that my program made from Chicago's blocked system. It had mellowed already, dropped in intensity and speed, which meant that the Sammy and his crew had stopped. Chicago was still in pain, but it was drawn out now, the music long and slow. Not the jangling horror show of nerves being ripped out, but the ache of injury, played like blues, deep and sorrowful.

"Oh baby, I'm sorry," I said, looking out at my city, at the river and the lights and buildings, the farm and people, one million

million things all humming together in the night like one big restless animal. "I didn't know."

I hadn't, and I'd let Sammy sucker me in, and I'd trashed my life and caused my city this pain, but I'd learned something else tonight. My program, my little scramble for funds that I had just about given up on, had proven itself. Not because it found out what Sammy was up too, any diagnostic could have done that. But a diagnostic program wouldn't have screamed, wouldn't have made music that caught my heart and made me feel bad for what was happening.

Sammy was right. My program had made me care. Without it, if I had just known what he was doing, just had someone tell me he was scrapping, I might have done what Sammy suggested, turned a blind eye and took my funds. It was just pipe, just wire.

Just my conscience, so easily silenced.

With the music though…

"Caring. That's something good, right Bunny? Even if it's for a thing, like a city, or you?"

"Yep yep," she said cheerfully, and I smiled, and tore that stupid play-dough off the circuits on the wall, letting Chicago's blues pour out, into the system.

Gary Kloster is a writer, a stay-at-home father, a martial artist, and a librarian. Sometimes all in the same day, seldom all at the same time. He lives in a college town in the midwest with his wife, daughters, and disgruntled cats. His first book, *Firesoul,* is available now.

The Drowned City
Bo Balder

The train from New Sydney turned onto the long bridge connecting the Western Australian mainland with the island of New Amsterdam. Jones opened the compartment window to see better and to sniff the sea air. After the two-day journey through deserts and eucalyptus forests, this was her first view of the rebuilt city. The train slid into a covered railway station constructed from red bricks. High arches vaulted the doorways, ornamented with yellow bricks and signs in a foreign language. She knew it must be Dutch, but she'd only ever spoken it as a child, and hadn't learned to read and write properly until after she'd immigrated to Australia.

She'd been asked to head the evaluation team for a grand project the Dutch were proposing, an extension of the city they'd already created in the ocean. A prestigious task, and one that would cement her growing reputation as a crisis manager and problem solver. Her job was to stop the project, as it was threatening to use up more than its share of resources. She'd read about the poor Europeans. Some countries there had lost so many coastal lands in the rising sea levels that they'd been cut in half, like the Netherlands. Australia had offered the homeless Dutch a piece of Australia as an alternative to moving to neighboring countries in Europe. Australia needed the citizens after the great die-off, and many Dutch people didn't want to become Germans or Belgians, for patriotic reasons Jones hadn't quite grasped.

Jones would be visiting people who'd clung to their old culture so hard they'd wrestled new land out of the sea, as they apparently had been doing for centuries, only now in the warm coastal waters just off Cape Le Grand. Jones had been tasked with evaluating and probably terminating the project. Her own Dutch roots, shallow as they might be, had played a role in her selection. All she knew of that part of her background were the few faded pictures her opa had grudgingly shown her when he was sober.

As she got out of the train and left the station, the air smelled of salt and old stone. It hadn't been possible, or allowed, to recreate the temperate West-European climate of old Amsterdam, but she'd seen pictures of the old city and the trees looked exactly the same, even though they had to be engineered native species.

She'd try to reserve judgment. She really would. But still. You wouldn't catch her recreating the rotting plastic refinery in the Pacific Gyre where she'd grown up, ever. Why hang onto the past?

She was about to cross a wide bridge over a canal, her eye caught by the white glass-covered boats that lay at anchor, when she heard someone calling her name.

"Ms. de Vries! Ms. de Vries!"

A man was trying to reach her through the exiting crowd, holding a big white placard with "Jones de Vries" lettered on it.

He arrived and held out his hand. "Aalt de Vries, *aangenaam*."

Jones clasped the hand and answered in English. "Jones, also de Vries, nice to meet you. I'm sorry, my Dutch is kind of rusty."

"That's okay. I have to say, you look very Dutch. You'll fit right in with your long legs and your blond hair."

"I thought Dutch people were white," Jones said. Her warm gold skin suddenly stood out, as it didn't in New Sydney.

"Originally, sure," Aalt said. "But look at me, I'm at least half Korean."

"And one of my grandmothers was from Indonesia," Jones said. She smiled at Aalt. He seemed familiar, in spite of his accent and formal clothes.

For now, she was enjoying the stroll over the Damrak. It looked exactly like the old pictures she'd looked up on the train. The buildings lining it seemed to be from a wildly varying array of building styles and ages of origin. She guessed that was how cities grew, adding one house at a time. New Sydney was the only city she knew well, and it looked nothing like this, except maybe a few buildings in the historical center. New Amsterdam looked like cities had before the Drowning and the epidemics. People didn't build this extravagantly anymore for private use. Communal living had been on the rise for decades.

A fine mist drizzled on her face. It was kind of pleasant.

"How is it raining here? This coast hardly gets any rain."

"Global warming changed all the weather systems, so this bit of Australia is going to end up as rainforest in a couple of centuries, we think. But the change isn't far enough advanced that we can depend on that. We made a sprinkler system. Too risky to mess with real clouds."

"Where are we going?" she asked Aalt.

"To the Palace, to meet our project managers for a presentation."

"Palace? Like with a king or queen?"

Aalt's face tightened slightly. "Used to be. But they've stayed in the old country."

Jones grimaced mentally. "I'm sorry, I'm realizing I know little about the Netherlands. I know that you had to abandon half the country because of the sea levels rising, and that you created new land in the sea. Tell me more how this all happened, and you know, if these buildings are copies, or the actual thing."

Aalt's shoulders relaxed. While he filled Jones in on the gigantic project, Jones took in the quaint gables, the irregular old bricks, and the people strolling past. Their height and build did remind her of herself, although she hadn't been in a place with white people making up such a large percentage of the population before. White faces and blond hair were everywhere. Very odd.

"You have to understand the psychological blow of losing your hometown, your home province, half your country. The gift of this location was of course a wonderful gesture of the Australian government, but I think if we hadn't started shaping it into the image of the Netherlands, we would have seen much depression and many suicides. This project gave people a reason to hang on, to go on living and building and dreaming."

Being landless, being lost and despairing, she knew what that felt like. She'd hated life aboard the floating plastic factory, and had left as soon as she could for Australia. "Where were your people from, in the old country?" Aalt asked. "Is it still there?"

Jones shook her head. "No, we were from the North, I think, a fishing town. I guess that's why my opa was so angry all the time. It was all gone."

Aalt put his hand on Jones' arm. "If you know the name, we could go and visit."

That was kind of him. Jones racked her brain. She wasn't sure if she could go find this information online, since her grandfather had lived his life defiantly without everything automated beyond the phone and the fridge. "I think, Hark? Harbinger?"

"Could it be Harlingen?" Aalt pronounced it just like opa had.

"Yeah! Did you guys recreate it?"

"We didn't, although we'd love to. That's why you're here. Harlingen's a gorgeous old town. But we can let you visit our virtual recreation."

"Sure, I'd love to."

Aalt gestured to a blocky grey building, old looking. "The Palace."

Jones looked up at the gigantic edifice. Not as nice as the brick canal houses. Office-like, in fact.

They entered through carved wooden doors. Jones couldn't stop herself. "Is this real wood?" She was prepared to be scandalized by the use of world's lung tissue. The forests and jungles around the world still hadn't recovered completely from the devastation human felling and global warming had caused.

"Yes, but its ancient wood. Isn't it better to honor wood that was felled in a less fragile time, than not use it? What would happen to it?"

Jones stuck out her hand to touch it. It felt just like printed wood. But he was right. The tree it had been cut from was from an era with plenty of trees.

After a short trip in an elevator and some narrow hallways, Aalt preceded her into a large meeting room. Tall pale people in formal dress sat around an oval table. The atmosphere was heavy and Jones was starting to feel underdressed. The temperatures here in the West weren't really much different from Sydney, but everybody dressed as if it was winter. Long sleeves, long pants, closed shoes. Somebody should have briefed her.

The oldest of the suited men stood up and stuck out his hand. Jones shook it, bemused. He spoke to her in a language she couldn't parse, at first. Just her surname, de Vries, stood out. He pronounced it like her grandfather did. With a few seconds delay, the meaning of the murmured words swam up from deep memory. He'd just said nice to meet her. She could have guessed that without having a knowledge of spoken Dutch.

"Goedemorgen," Jones said, the harsh gutturals coming back with some difficulty. Felt like she was clearing her throat. But she was pretty sure that was the total extent of her formal Dutch. She might still have been able to uphold a conversation about fishing or plastic refining, but that was it. "I'm sorry, my Dutch is too rusty for a business meeting. I only spoke it occasionally, as a child."

"We were promised a Dutch-speaking, Dutch heritage representative," the chairman said, his Dutch accent flattening the words.

Another man spoke. "It's not that important, Verhagen, we can tell her in English."

Jones kept her face impassive. They could talk about her all they wanted, she didn't care. Her experience as ambassador had turned her mostly immune to rudeness; it usually came down to cultural differences.

Verhagen turned to Jones again. "Have a seat, mevrouw de Vries."

Jones sat down and smiled her friendliest smile. "Thank you, meneer Verhagen. Tell me about your proposal. "

Jones only half-listened to their elaborate proposal, complete with mock-ups of the expansion of New Amsterdam. Her eye camera would record everything anyway. It was more important to get the emotional feel of the room, get a handle on the internal tension, their hopes, the things they weren't saying.

Why did they cling so hard to their past glory? What was wrong with Australia's existing cities? Old Amsterdam had been a gorgeous city, and she was sure the thousands of years of history of the Dutch countryside had been a loss. But it seemed wasteful and indulgent to try and make a literal copy. For what purpose?

After the presentation, the Dutch held a dinner for the evaluation team. Jones was expecting the usual rice and beans with a few locally grown vegetables, but the spread seemed imported straight from a history book. Bread, apples, pears, temperate climate fruits she'd never eaten before.

Servers carried in a large platter covered with a domed silver cover. Jones felt a frisson of fear. Surely they wouldn't offer her meat? She'd heard that horrible habit of meat eating was rife among these ex-Europeans, and she'd be in a hell of a pickle. Either she'd offend her hosts by declining the course, or she'd taint herself by eating dead mammals.

The lid lifted and was shown to be a complicated vegetable pie creation.

Jones blew out a relieved breath.

"What did you think it was going to be?" said her neighbor, one of the Dutch members of the project.

Do not offend thine host, Jones said to herself. She smiled as best she could. "We don't usually get these kinds of food in New Sydney. I wasn't sure I'd like it."

The young man's eyebrows rose. "Like what, meat? We know you're all vegetarians."

"Implying you're not?"

He gave a European kind of ambiguous shrug. "We're open about all types of food."

Jones just didn't want to know. Killing fellow creatures was primitive, repulsive, and keeping them was bad for the climate. She wished they'd seated her next to Aalt, who'd seemed easier to get along with.

The young man, who was very handsome, kept asking questions, smiling too widely and being upset at her answers, which apparently weren't the ones he expected. "How can you say the marine environment is more important than hundreds of thousands of people!"

"I'm still making up my mind," Jones said and took a large bite of her food so that he couldn't press her further.

Jones turned to her neighbor on the right, an older woman in a full suit and high-necked blouse. The woman glared at her. "I hope the Australian government realizes how important the rebuilding of Amsterdam is for the Dutch."

Jones smiled and complimented her on the authentic taste of Dutch raw herring.

After dessert, Aalt sidled up to Jones. "If you're still interested, you could get that virtual tour of Harlingen right now."

Jones jumped at the chance to leave the tense atmosphere of the dining room. Too many people hoping she'd vote for their project, or afraid that she might not. Solitude was just what she needed, even if it was virtual.

**

Jones strapped in at the VR facility in the Palace. She closed her eyes and surrendered to the simulation.

A train rode through orderly, bright green country. Black and white pied cows grazed blissfully in the ruler-straight meadows. Jones looked them up. Had the Dutch really kept that much cattle, shooting out CO_2 and methane like there was no tomorrow? They had. But in the project, the Dutch had promised the cows would be holograms.

The train passed through adorable little villages, green meadows, and the occasional patch of undeveloped white space.

Two and half hours later, subjective time, she got out on a windy train platform.

Apart from one surly old person who pretended not to speak English, Harlingen appeared deserted. Maybe everyone was meant to be out working, or maybe they hadn't populated the simulation yet.

Jones followed her inphone's direction through narrow, cobbled streets. She peered inside one of the toy houses to see if it was inhabited, but net curtains and rows of plants prevented her from seeing in.

It was only a ten minute walk to the edge of the sea.

She stared. It looked like a real sea, it smelled like a real sea, only it was a darker grey green than Sydney's inviting blue waters. More like the Northern Pacific. She found stairs leading right to the water's edge, and dipped her hand it. Yup. Good simulation, maybe a bit warm, not as freezing as it looked.

Someone coughed. She discovered a man in odd clothes standing next to her. He wore wide wool pants, a patched, tight sweater, and a dark blue wool cap, very authentic-looking, and unflattering. He took off his cap and wiped sweat off his graying blond hair. His face reminded her of her grandfather's long, stern planes and narrow light eyes.

"Are you a real person?" she asked.

"I'm Aalt."

"Hi! Does this look like the real North Sea?"

He spit out something horrible and dark brown. "Real enough. Smell could use some work though, but they don't want to put the visitors off."

Jones wrinkled her nose. If the smell of rotting seaweed got any stronger, she'd wake up from the simulation retching. "How are you going to make this real if you get the funding?"

"We'll create new dykes and fill in the land. We call it polders. We'll put a ring wall out in the ocean, which we'll paint and cover with holographic projections. Sound effects, wave makers, the whole shebang."

"That's insane. Think of all that power you'll be spending! And the sea here looks just fine to me."

He shrugged. "It's not the North Sea. And it'll be solar energy, not to worry. We're not burning coal or anything. This is what it would look like in reality."

The waves smoothed out. The sea became less noisy, and something at the horizon flickered. Jones could see the retaining walls now. The blue-grey paint was nice, but the bright blue Australian sky behind it kind of spoiled the effect.

"It still feels wasteful."

"I bet you were raised by Dutch people!"

"I told you my grandfather was from Harlingen."

"Welcome home, then. What was his name?"

"Sieuwert de Vries."

He smiled widened. "That's my grandpa's surname, too."

"Is it a rare name?" Jones asked. "Are we family?"

She kind of wanted him to be.

"I think we are. My grandfather was called Jacob and his brother was named Sieuwert."

Jones heart skipped a beat. "What the- we're really cousins?"

"I guess. Hey, cousin Jones!"

He did look like her grandfather here. Not her father, he'd taken after the Indonesian side, her grandmother's. But no, she'd seen Aalt's real face, his half-Asian face. This was a simulation.

The longer she looked at her newly discovered cousin, Aalt, the weirder she felt. A bit light-headed, and with the oddest lump in her throat. Best distract herself away from it by looking at the fake sea.

"Tell me, really, why are you people doing this? Why can't the Dutch just immigrate and become Australian like everyone else? "

Cousin Aalt got an earnest look on his face. "This isn't a whim, Jones. This isn't a plaything for idle, bored people. Our heritage matters to us. It's shaped us. We are who we are because of the climate we grew up in, because of the landscape. Let me show you."

They turned away from the sea.

"Yeah, so, why then immigrate to this hot, arid piece of Australia instead of staying close to your roots? What's wrong with the eastern Netherlands, or Germany?"

"We have a difference of opinion with them."

Jones laughed. "They thought this was a silly plan as well? Sound like my kind of people."

Cousin Aalt halted before a large, low building built of brick. "This is my elementary school. See that canal? That's where our grandfathers used to skate from their farm to school in winter. In my time, global warming had made that impossible. But still. The canal was there."

"So my opa went to school here as well?"

"Yup."

Jones walked up to one of the windows and peeked in. It seemed like a terrible way to lock children up, sitting in rows, staring at the blackboard. Jones wasn't sure that such outdated education methods deserved re-introduction.

"Get in the boat," Cousin Aalt called out. She turned to find him standing in a small, flat-bottomed boat, pole in hand.

Jones didn't like water, never had, ever since a near-drowning in the churning North Pacific in deepest winter, but this was not only a glassy smooth canal, it was a simulation.

"All right."

"I'll pole you to opa's family farm."

"Wasn't he a fisherman?"

"No. The younger sons went into fishing, the eldest took over the farm. He was the eldest. I think it went bust and he had to get a job on the plastic refinery."

Cousin Aalt poled them over the canal, through green flat pastures with simulated cows in them. The red-roofed farmhouses looked low and impossibly picturesque.

"Did people really live there?" Jones asked.

"They really did."

Jones had been raised on the plastic factory, where no attention at all had been paid to aesthetics, and lived in New Sydney, where it was mild and sunny all the year round and people built their own open, wooden houses with kitchen gardens to eke out the rice and beans.

"What's all this space for? It looks so empty."

"Cows mostly, for their milk. Wheat, corn, oats, potatoes."

Things Jones had never seen or eaten in her life, until lunch today. Temperate climate foods, twentieth century foods that could no longer be cultivated in the hot, moist world of today.

"Let's go inside." They clambered off the boat and crossed the yard.

Jones followed Aalt. The door opened into a tiny hallway, which made sense in a cooler climate, to keep the heat of the house in. It smelled funny, of mold, wool, mud, animals, people.

Aalt gestured her into a kitchen. Everything seemed so antiquated. Yes, there was a fridge, but it didn't have a readout, no screens, no food machine. Lots of space for cooking, cutting, and storing foodstuff though.

They walked through to a sitting room, with a rustic, tile-covered fireplace. The mantelpiece held a row of pictures.

Jones bent forward to study them, fighting the urge to just enlarge them with a tap. She wanted to keep pretending this wasn't a simulation. She kind of recognized the faces of the people in the photograph. Not just her opa, but his brother and his father, they all looked so alike. To be honest, they looked like the face she saw in the mirror every morning, if you disregarded the skin color, the folded eyelids and the tight curls of her hair. They looked like family.

Her cheeks burned. Her eyes prickled. She turned away from

cousin Aalt to hide the emotion. For god's sake, why would this hit her so? She knew the project was trying to rope her in.

"Just for the record, I resent being manipulated this blatantly. Showing me my own roots so I'd vote for you." The anger was helping her put the emotion aside.

Cousin Aalt, who felt like her cousin even though he might not really be, grimaced apologetically. "Sorry. But is it working?"

"What do you think? This is nice and all, but it doesn't change my mind. You're not my real cousin either!"

His face fell. He'd really expected it to work.

"Let's go back to New Amsterdam," Jones said. "I'm not going to get any more convinced."

Her hand moved up to the exit button behind her ear.

The real Aalt surged up from his chair as she stormed out of the simulation center. No time to wait for the elevator, down the stairs, out, she needed fresh air.

She walked out of the Palace and took the first right, a narrow, curved street hemmed in by old looking buildings that had shops on the ground floor. Her stomach churned with emotion. She tried to name them, as her mandatory immigration therapy had taught her. Anger, definitely. At dredging up her opa's life, trying to make her feel. At the reality of opa's sad, fucked up life, which in his turn had caused him to fuck up his son and granddaughter. It had made Jones run as far away from the plastic refinery as she could, and now she saw she'd just been replaying opa's running away from his parents' farm.

A big screen flickered to her left. She halted to take it in. It seemed to show the building the screen was attached to, only blurry and grayed out. Or no, it was under water, the ruins of the building right here. Which must be a copy. It was a webcam showing this very same building as it was right now, under the waves of the North Sea, half buried under silt and other debris. Jones stood transfixed and watched seaweed wave and a shoal of small grey fish flicker by.

So this must be what her opa's real farm looked like now. Buried, flooded, collapsed. Gone, forever.

Tears burned in her eyes.

She couldn't stand looking at the screen any longer and turned away. More than half of the buildings in the street had similar screens. Some didn't. Those must be the real old buildings, the best ones for some reason, that had gotten packed up and transported here, half a world away.

She stuck out a hand and touched a column of ornamental brickwork. The bricks looked irregular, handmade. So in the past, a brickmaker had baked this brick, a bricklayer had picked it up from a stack and mortared it in. People had lived in this building, died, borne children. It was real. The rough texture of the brick against her hand was real.

She wished with all her heart that she could feel the actual brick of her grandfather's old house. Or even that she had one of these old photos of his. Or that any of her family was still alive so she could call them and hear their voice.

"You all right, lady?" a voice said behind her back.

Jones startled and wiped her face. "Fine, thank you."

She turned away and started walking back to the palace.

Her opa might have walked these very stones. Every cobble, every defunct traffic light made her weepy and silent. To tread where her ancestors had. To touch a stone they'd hewn with their own long-dead hands.

She was going to support the Dutch project to preserve their heritage. She couldn't deny anyone that experience.

Bo Balder is the first Dutch author to have published a story in the famous F&SF(Fantasy & Science Fiction magazine), Sept/Oct 2015. Her other short fiction has appeared in Crossed Genres (#35 Anticipation) and quite a few anthologies. Her sf novel "The Wan" will be published fall 2015 by Pink Narcissus Press. She attended Viable Paradise and is a member of Codex Writers Group.

Bo lives and works close to Amsterdam, Europe. When she isn't writing, you can find her madly designing knitwear, painting, and reading everything from Kate Elliott to Iain M. Banks or Jared Diamond."

SCI FUTURES

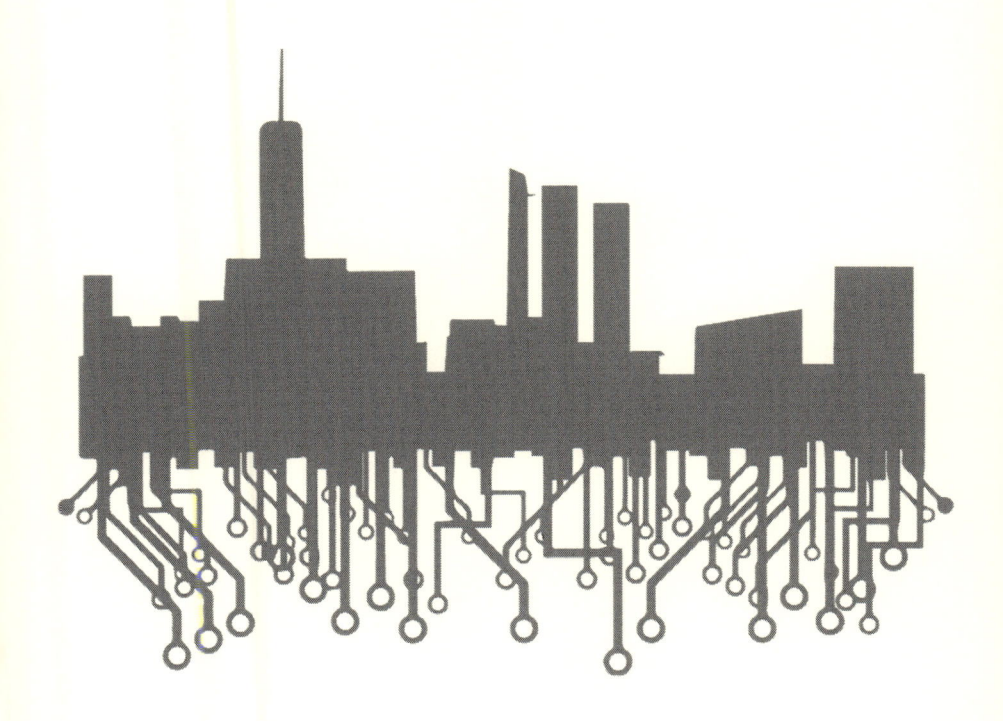

Printed in Great Britain
by Amazon